Tempted by the Prince

The Raminar Family

Elizabeth Lennox

Copyright 2021
ISBN13: 9798703323847
All rights reserved

This is a work of fiction. Names, characters, businesses, places, events, and incidents are either the product of the author's imagination or used in a fictitious manner. Any resemblance to actual persons, living or dead, or actual events is purely coincidental. Any duplication of this material, either electronic or any other format, either currently in use or a future invention, is strictly prohibited, unless you have the direct consent of the author.

Table of Contents

CHAPTER 1   1

CHAPTER 2   10

CHAPTER 3   17

CHAPTER 4   22

CHAPTER 5   30

CHAPTER 6   37

CHAPTER 7   47

CHAPTER 8   55

CHAPTER 9   60

CHAPTER 10   71

CHAPTER 11   78

CHAPTER 12   80

CHAPTER 13   88

CHAPTER 14   93

EPILOGUE   101

EXCERPT FOR ONE MORE KISS   104

Chapter 1

"You want...*what*?!" Rachel asked, trying to hide the panic that was filling her throat.

Princess Talia, Rachel's boss, smiled as she patted her infant son's bottom, the little guy was fast asleep in her arms and adorably cute. "My brother wants to build a university. He needs someone who understands the details, knows how to get things done, and is reliable and trustworthy. That's you, Rachel. You've been an incredible assistant and are amazing at organizing everything and knowing what has to happen. You're perfect for the job."

Inwardly, Rachel cringed. "Trustworthy". Yep, that was her. She was reliable and trustworthy. Loyal. Hardworking.

Her boss and good friend could have described a golden retriever with the same adjectives. Rachel fought not to show how much those words hurt.

Rachel looked down at her gathered, flowered skirt that she'd paired with a high-necked silk blouse and wished she looked less...frumpy. She compared herself to Talia who, even post-partum, looked gloriously beautiful in a blue cotton dress that hugged her breasts then draped lovingly over her still-plump belly. In contrast, Rachel was just...ordinary. Her only saving grace, her green eyes, were overwhelmed by her hair. She couldn't seem to tame it. The wild spirals had a mind of their own and nothing she'd tried in the past could smooth them out. Oh, how she'd love to have silky, dark, smooth hair like Talia's! Rachel couldn't help but admire the way Talia's hair cascaded over her shoulders, looking sleek and sophisticated.

As Rachel watched Talia sooth her newborn son back to sleep, that wistful stab of envy gnawed at her. Rachel was twenty-six years old and had been working with Princess Talia for a while now. But what about her hopes for a child? For a family? She worked long hours, ensuring that the princess's schedule ran smoothly, running interception on anything that might clog up the day's plans, and resolved crises before they happened. That left little time for dating and romance.

Not that she'd had a great deal of romance before taking this job! And in truth, she absolutely loved working for Talia. The hard work was a breeze compared to what she'd done before coming here.

No, the issue wasn't the job or the long hours. It was…that niggling sense that life was passing her by. That she'd never find the time to have a life dictated by her own terms, a life centered around her family and her children. Often, Rachel felt as if she were sitting on the sidelines, watching everyone else be happy and find their dreams, falling in love and having precious babies.

The idea of Tarin being the father of her children popped into her mind. But that image wasn't new. In fact, it had occurred to her so many times that she was used to pushing it away.

The idea of helping Talia's brother with a project as massive as building a university was an amazing opportunity, Rachel told herself.

However, no matter how amazing the opportunity or exciting the challenge, Rachel couldn't take on this project for one excellent reason.

She was in love with Prince Tarin.

Embarrassing and heart-wrenching to admit, not to mention trite and predictable. And yet, still true. There was no way Rachel could work side by side for the man again! She'd done it for a few months after Princess Talia's marriage to Sheik Santos of Padar. But after the princess' wedding, Talia had worked mostly here in Padar, and Rachel had worked very hard to stifle, or at least ignore, her feelings for the handsome prince. For a while now, she'd been successful at ignoring her painful, unrequited love for the tall, amazingly handsome, virile, gorgeous, and funny prince.

So no. Work directly for the man? She just couldn't do it!

Shifting slightly in the comfortable chair, Rachel folded her hands over her lap, trying to appear calm. "Thank you so much for the compliment," she said, pulling her shoulders back, "but I already have a job, Your Highness. I work for you."

Talia grinned, her eyes lighting up. "That's the best part! I'm taking some time off." She looked down at her two week old son. "I know that I worked right after giving birth to Sinan," she explained, referring to her first son, "but this time, I'm going to take off more time. No interviews, no light duty." She sighed and leaned back slightly, staring lovingly at her infant son. "I really pushed too hard after Sinan's birth two years ago. I told Santos that I wanted to slow down this time. He even agreed to slow down with me and has already delegated more than half of his responsibilities to his staff for the next several months. So both of us are taking time off in order to be with our kids."

Rachel swallowed past the lump of envy that threatened to choke her. "That sounds wonderful," she whispered, then cleared her throat to allay the worry in Talia's eyes. "I'm so happy for both of you."

Princess Talia's smile brightened. "Then it's settled. You'll work with Tarin for the next several months and I'll enjoy being a momma. Then we'll meet back here in three months and start over. Sounds good, right?!"

Rachel thought hard, but she couldn't come up with any alternatives besides quitting. But since she absolutely loved her job, loved working with Princess Talia, she pressed her lips together, suppressing the urge to beg Her Highness not to throw her to the wolf!

Rachel stood up and walked out of the room on numb legs, frantically trying to come up with a plan. Any plan! Anything that would keep her from being around Prince Tarin el Raminar, the most amazingly wonderful, sweetly kind man she'd ever met in her life!

Just being on the opposite side of the room from him had once sent her heart fluttering and she'd dropped her armload of papers. Thankfully, he'd been too far away to notice what was happening, but she'd learned her lesson that day.

Tarin closed his eyes as he dropped his phone on the desk. Looking outside at the small, sun-filled courtyard, he breathed slowly in, held the breath for a few seconds, then released the air in a controlled manner. He'd learned the technique after training with the US Navy SEALs and it had served him well over the years.

Unfortunately, the SEALs had never met Rachel Morris. The breathing technique didn't help in any way and his body tightened just thinking about the woman's delicate features and her soft curves, which she always kept hidden beneath the most hideous outfits. Unfortunately, those dresses were more like some sort of virginal fetish-wear, he thought, leaning his hands against his desk and bowing his head. She was so incredibly lovely in a soft, delicate way.

She was beautiful, but he couldn't say that Rachel was the most beautiful woman he'd ever seen, but there was just something about her, something that called to him. She could be just walking down the hallway and when he'd see her, his body would tighten with desire as he watched those flowered, librarian/school-teacher dresses flutter around her legs. Every time she pushed those dark-rimmed glasses higher up onto her nose, it felt like she was touching his...!

"Damn it!" he snapped.

"What the hell is wrong with you?" his brother, Gaelen, asked. Gaelen was about eighteen months younger than their oldest brother, Amit, who was the leader of Izara, and every time a birthday came around, Tarin thanked God for their birth order! The thought of what Amit had to deal with every damn day would leave Tarin begging for mercy. Amit released the tension from his oppressive responsibilities by drawing and, lately, painting. He was pretty damn good too.

But Tarin enjoyed being responsible for the infrastructure of Izara. He loved inspecting bridges and buildings, commissioning road projects and water systems. The job called to his long passion of architecture and suited his personality perfectly.

Gaelen dropped a file on his desk. "These are the consultants you asked me about last week."

Tarin looked at the thick folder and groaned. Just the thought of going through all those reports made his shoulder muscles tighten, because he knew that he should hand off the task to his assistant. And he would... as soon as the lovely, shockingly sexy Rachel arrived. Which would be in...he looked at his watch and sighed...two days, four hours, and sixteen minutes.

"I heard that Rachel is coming back to take care of this mess," Galen continued, slouching into one of the leather chairs in front of Tarin's desk.

Tarin turned away, frustrated beyond measure. "Right. I just got off the phone with Talia."

"So, when is Rachel arriving?"

Tarin had the sudden urge to punch his older brother. Not for any valid reason. Just because he couldn't handle the almost unrelenting desire that he'd be forced to endure as soon as Rachel arrived. "I don't know," he lied.

Gaelen chuckled, and once again, Tarin ignored him.

His brother slapped his knees as if he'd just had a brilliant idea. "Well, hang in there. Rachel will get here soon and she'll fix all of this stuff, organize it into a well-oiled project machine."

With that, Gaelen pushed out of the chair and walked out of Tarin's office.

"Yeah, that's what I'm afraid of," he muttered.

"What the hell are you afraid of?"

Tarin leaned his head back in frustration as Amit, his oldest brother, walked in. "What do you want?" he demanded with absolutely no respect for his brother, despite him being the Sheik of their fair country.

Amit chuckled and Tarin turned to find his brother leaning in the doorway, his arms crossed over his chest. "I heard that Rachel was coming back. Any word on when she'll arrive?"

Once again, Tarin had to restrain the urge to swing. Physical release might be exactly what he needed right now. But Amit didn't deserve it, and besides, there was only a fifty percent chance that Tarin's fist would connect.

"I have no idea. I just got off the phone with Talia. Rachel will need an apartment, arrange to have all of her furniture moved back here, pack up her house, and..."

"She shouldn't have to worry about all that. Just put her in one of the executive apartments. That's why we have them, after all. They are fully furnished, two bedroom apartments. Rachel would just need to pack up her clothes and she could be here tonight."

Tarin glared at Amit, but his older brother only smiled. Amit didn't used to be this happy. He used to be the grump of the family. That was before Harper, his wife and the mother of his two children, arrived and told the ass to get over himself.

"That's a good idea," he grumbled, but didn't pick up the phone to make the call. The longer he could delay Rachel's arrival, the better. He needed time to mentally prepare.

Apparently, Amit wasn't going to give him that time, the bastard! "I'll have Rashid work out the details. We'll fly her up in the private jet tonight, so she doesn't have to take a commercial flight." With that, Amit left, whistling annoyingly.

Tarin glared daggers at his older brother's back, wishing that he could come up with a viable reason to stop him. But everything Amit had said made perfect sense and was actually far more convenient for Rachel. If she'd had to find her own apartment, she'd need to look around for at least a weekend. And because Rachel was so careful, she'd look at several apartments before making a decision. She'd weigh the pros and cons of each building and the property's amenities, calculate the commute time, and locate the grocery stores and dry cleaners in the area. He smiled, knowing that Rachel would even drive to her preferred location at night, listen for sounds, walk the streets to make sure she felt safe and comfortable.

Rachel was one of the most detail oriented women he'd ever met. If she hadn't been so loyal to Talia, and if Tarin didn't lust after her so badly, he would have tried to steal Rachel away from his baby sister by now. But having Rachel around was...painful. She was so damn beautiful and everything about her, from the way she smiled to the way she walked...it all turned him on! Before she'd moved to Padar after Talia married that ass Santos, Tarin had been in an almost constant state of arousal, just because he'd see Rachel around the palace hallways.

So, what the hell was he going to do now? Rachel would be on a plane, most likely by tonight and, because she was such a dedicated employee, she'd report to work in the morning.

"Hell!" he groaned and turned around.

He remembered the first time he'd seen her. She had been so shy, so tentative and worried that she'd mess up somehow. Talia had raved about Rachel's brilliance from day one. When he'd stepped into Talia's office during the first week of Rachel's employment, he'd seen her drop papers, break a pencil, spill coffee all over her desk, and even trip over her chair.

When she'd looked up at him with those huge, green eyes, blinking back tears of embarrassment, he'd smiled, trying to ease her fears. "It's going to be okay," he'd told her gently.

Even then, he'd felt something. It had been strange, like a tingling sensation that had started in his groin. Tarin had tried to ignore it. Rachel was pretty, with delicate features, beautiful green eyes, and hair that...damn, his fingers ached to explore those auburn curls, to see if they were soft or coarse, to twirl one around his finger and see how long her hair really was.

But her hideous flowered dress with the lace around the neck and the full skirt wasn't anything to draw a man's eye. She was...pretty but... like a librarian. A sexy, naughty librarian!

That night, he'd had the most erotic dream of his entire life. He'd been taking off that flowered dress, stroking her soft, full thighs and... he'd woken in a cold sweat, his body rock hard and his muscles tight with lust. He'd looked around that night, searching for the soft, warm, female body. But his bed had been empty.

That had been two years ago. His bed had been empty ever since! Tarin had tried to find another woman, searched for someone that might temper this painful lust he felt for Rachel. But no other woman had tempted him even slightly. It was almost like...like Rachel's damn flowered skirts had ruined him for other women.

He cursed the fact that Rachel was coming back and he blamed his brothers for the speed at which his life was about to career out of control.

Rachel lugged her heavy suitcase out of the back of her small, eco-nomical SUV, dumping it onto the tarmac. "Ugh!" She took a deep breath. One of the ways she'd learned to deal with the intense heat of the desert climate here in Padar, which was similar to that of Izara, was to never work outside during the middle of the day. The cool mornings were lovely and the chilly evenings almost magical. But the heat of the afternoon was truly unbearable.

If she'd had her way, Rachel would be right back in her precious Atlanta, Georgia, where the grass was a soft green at this time of the year. The roses would be in full bloom and the air would be languid with the balmy summer breeze.

Pushing her sunglasses higher up her nose, she slapped a hand down on top of her annoying, floppy hat before it blew away. The gust of intensely hot air that threatened to take her hat with it wasn't a breeze. It was God's furnace.

"Good grief," she muttered, hitching her tote bag higher up onto her shoulder as she headed for the ridiculously large plane that was waiting for her, her suitcase rolling alongside.

An airport worker hurried over to her, his mirrored sunglasses hiding his eyes. "Are you Ms. Morris?" he yelled over the roar of the plane.

"Yes. That's me," she yelled back, leaning towards the man's ear to be heard.

He smiled and nodded. "I'll take that for you, ma'am. Go ahead and board the plane. We'll take off as soon as you're seated."

Startled, Rachel immediately handed over her cumbersome suitcase, wiping her hands on her flowered skirt. "Oh! I'm so sorry! I didn't mean to hold up the others." Rachel ignored the man's confused expression as she rushed across the hot cement towards the stairs that had been rolled up to the door of the plane. Grabbing onto the steel stair rail, she jerked her hand back with a hiss. The sun had heated the steel handrail until it was too hot to touch. "Darn it! Why did I do that?" As she raced up the stairs, Rachel gathered up her full skirt so that she didn't step on it, careful not to trip because she didn't want to grab the handrail again.

"Good afternoon, Ms. Morris," the flight attendant greeted her with a coolly professional smile. "We're ready whenever you are."

Rachel sighed with relief as the blessedly cool air of the plane caressed her overheated skin, and looked around, ready to smile her apologies to the other passengers. But the plane was empty. "Um...where's everyone else?" she asked, moving deeper into the divinely cool interior.

The flight attendant turned the lock on the plane's door. "You're our only passenger this trip," she announced. "Would you prefer a glass of champagne before takeoff?"

Rachel stared at the woman who looked like a perfectly made up Barbie doll in a flight attendant's crisp, beautiful uniform. The only difference between her uniform and that of another airline's was that hers had the Izara government seal on the sleeve.

"No, thank you. I'll just go sit over there and work during the flight."

The woman smiled as she nodded. "Take whatever seat you prefer. What would you like for dinner?"

Rachel started and looked back at her. "No! I don't...I mean, you don't need to bother with making a meal for me."

The woman's smile widened. "It's not a problem at all. It's a long flight and cooking meals helps pass the time. So it really isn't a bother in any way."

Rachel sighed. She didn't like people making a fuss over her. "Well, whatever you're having for dinner is fine."

The flight attendant tilted her head. "That's great. I'll tell the pilot that you're on board and she can take off anytime."

Sinking into one of the leather seats, Rachel sighed with relief once she was alone. Looking around, she studied the cabin. She remained in the section where the press would ride during the flights when accompanying a member of the royal family, although normally, she would ride in the back of the plane with Princess Talia. It was a much more comfortable area with wider seats, deep sofas, a conference room, and several bedrooms along with bathrooms complete with showers. It was luxury at a level Rachel had never conceived of before she'd started working for Princess Talia. These luxurious flights were one of the perks of her job, a job she loved with all her heart. Every day was different and challenging and she knew that she was good at it.

And yet, as she stared out the plane's window, her heart ached at what was to come. Maybe if she hadn't been so good at her job, Prince Tarin wouldn't have agreed to use her for this next project. She wouldn't be flying towards the man who made her heart race and she wouldn't be about to make a fool of herself. Again.

She remembered the time she'd first seen the man. Prince Tarin had walked into her office and smiled at her and every muscle in her body had just...stopped functioning. She'd been stunned by his handsome features, terrified by his height and brawn, then awed by his sweet, devastating charm. As she'd gotten to know him over the past two years, Rachel had discovered that the enormous man with outrageous muscles was actually a horrible tease! He'd walk into her office and wink at her just to see her blush. He'd bring her cookies and other treats, knowing that Rachel had a terrible sweet tooth. He would tease her, tell her horrible jokes, then wink at her when she covered her mouth to stop herself from laughing.

He was also the most annoying brother to Talia and Rachel had watched with envy as Prince Tarin would tickle or hug his sister in variously affectionate ways. He loved lifting her off her feet and squeezing her until she laughed and begged for mercy.

Having come from a family that never touched, hugged, or even voiced affection, Rachel had craved those moments of familial warmth.

Plus, watching him with his twin nieces or his nephews was like watching a man in heaven. Prince Tarin might be a horrific playboy, loving the ladies and always flirting, but when it came to his duties as an uncle, he was sweet and kind, wildly protective, and could spend hours playing with them, holding them, taking them in the pool, and had infinite patience teaching them to ride horses, ride their bikes, play games or even reading to them. In fact, there had been many times she'd passed by the nursery and caught Prince Tarin with a baby in his arms, reading or feeding or just rocking them to sleep.

Her heart ached during those moments and she blinked back the tears at the memories. "This is going to be painful," she muttered to herself. Not even the past two years of working in Padar had eased her love for the man. He visited Talia too often for her to completely get him out of her mind.

But she had a job to do, she reminded herself. So, instead of mulling over the inevitable heartache, Rachel opened her computer and got to work. There were several issues she needed to conclude for Talia so that the princess could enjoy her maternity leave. Then she read through the information on the plans for the new university that Prince Tarin had sent.

Several hours later, Rachel had pages of notes and her excitement over the project was overriding her dread. "I'll just focus on work issues and not on…" She looked up just as the flight attendant stepped out of the small galley kitchen, carrying a cup of tea.

"Thank you!" Rachel gushed, grateful for the small gesture of kindness.

"My pleasure," the flight attendant replied. "I'll have dinner ready in about an hour."

And then Rachel was alone again. Always alone, she thought, as she sipped her tea and looked out the window. She was the boring, dependable, almost invisible person who made things happen for others.

Chapter 2

"Have you seen Rachel?" Gaelen asked.

SMACK!

Tarin stared up at his brother, the matt underneath him barely absorbing the brunt of his fall. "That was a good one!" Amit called, walking over and peering down at Tarin.

Tarin growled as he lunged upwards, furious that his brother had distracted him.

"Damn, Gaelen, you've woken the beast!" Amit laughed, smacking Gaelen on the back hard enough to send a normal man flying. But the Raminar brothers weren't normal. Amit and Gaelen were about the same height at six feet, three inches, but as the youngest brother, Tarin must have gotten a bit of extra testosterone because he was six feet, four and a half inches. Plus he easily added muscle to his tall frame with his daily workouts. When they were younger, the brothers used to tease Tarin, calling him "The Hulk" because he was so big. Now they didn't tease him because he would flatten them, although Tarin knew that his brothers still used the old nickname when he wasn't around.

"Low blow," Tarin grumbled. But along with his extra height and brawn, he'd also gotten a smooth temperament. Of the three, Tarin was the most laid-back, easiest to tease, and...the fastest to get retribution.

This time however, his brothers' teasing remarks had hit a nerve. He looked around, his hands fisted on his hips. "She's back?" he asked.

The other two had gone back to sparring, but they answered in between seemingly harsh blows.

"I heard from Rashid that she checked into the apartment late last night," Amit confirmed as he circled Gaelen, referring to the set of royal apartments set aside for diplomats or special guests. Or in Rachel's situation, for someone working on a special assignment as a favor to the palace.

Gaelen didn't even glance in Tarin's direction as he circled their oldest brother. "I heard she's wearing a pretty flowered dress this morning."

Tarin rolled his eyes. "She's *always* wearing a pretty flowered dress, you ass!"

Instead of wading into the fray, he headed towards the showers. "I have things to do. You boys can play around if you want."

The older two brothers stopped circling and straightened to watch their youngest brother head for the locker room. "He's got it bad," Amit muttered.

Gaelen nodded, smiling smugly. "Oh yeah. He's smitten."

Amit punched Gaelen's shoulder playfully. "Excellent idea bringing her back here."

Galen shrugged, and moved back into position for another round. "The idiot would have gone on moping around here if we hadn't done something. At least now he has a chance with her."

"If he doesn't mess it up," Amit agreed, then with lightning fast reflexes, moved in and tried to flip Gaelen over. He almost had him too, but Gaelen anticipated the effort and shifted his weight to the left, throwing Amit off balance. Heavy thuds echoed through the room as they pounded each other.

An hour later, Tarin adjusted the cuffs of his suit as he walked towards his office, his body alive and alert, ready to tackle the world. Or if not the world, at least one slight, delicately boned, beautiful, and elusive lady with magical curls and huge, green eyes, he thought.

Turning the corner, he only half listened as someone came up to him and asked for guidance on a bridge under construction. As Minister of the Interior, Tarin was ultimately responsible for every bridge, road, water system, and electricity grid within the country. He was in charge of ensuring their safety and building new infrastructure systems when needed.

And this latest project might not be completely within his area of responsibility, but he'd happily taken on the task when it was suggested last month. Even better, after his initial grumbling, Tarin was eager to work with Rachel on the project. She was a hell of a detail person, amazing at organizing everything and...!

She was pulling her stockings up.

Tarin stood in the doorway, admiring Rachel's very long, very sexy leg. Her flowered skirt was pulled all the way up to the top of her thigh. Tarin could clearly see the black lace of her garters holding up the taupe stockings. Holy hell! The demure, overly-efficient, flowered skirt was covering sex-kitten stockings and garters?!

Her legs were even sexier than he'd imagined. And he'd imagined a lot! Never, not in any of his dreams, either awake or sleeping, had he pictured her wearing stockings and garters! Cotton panties? Yep! And damn it, he'd thought even those would be sexy on Rachel! Cotton bra with no lace or any sort of accessory? Oh yeah! He'd thought himself a sick puppy when he'd considered that hot!

But silk stockings held up by a lacy garter?

Tarin watched as her long, delicate fingers slid her stockings up, as if they'd sunk down her legs somehow. She unattached the black clasp and reattached the stockings in a different place, the garter holding those sex-fantasy-things up against her pale skin.

Breathe, he reminded himself as he backed away into the hallway. Closing his eyes, he tilted his head back, clenching his fists as he took in deep gulps of air.

"She didn't know I was there," he told himself. "She thought she was alone!"

Damn it! He took several more breaths, trying to get himself back under control. It was difficult though, because keeping his eyes closed meant that he kept picturing her delicate hands sliding along her legs... her long, slender fingers doing that sexy thing with the clasps. Damn, how many times had he taken stockings off women in the past? Or left them on? Hell, he loved feeling stockings on a woman when he made love to her.

But never had he ever considered that Rachel would wear anything like that! Never! No way! He was almost angry about his discovery, because it would only add a whole new level of pain to his desire!

"What the hell is wrong with you?"

Tarin's eyes flew open and he found Amit standing in front of him.

"Go to hell," he snapped, his normal laid-back manner obliterated because of long, slim fingers gliding against silk stockings. And garters! He couldn't forget the damn garters!

Turning, he knocked on the wood panel of the doorframe before he entered Rachel's office this time. But instead of finding Rachel sitting behind her desk with her skirt pulled up and her leg slanted sideways, he noticed her standing up, looking for a file in a stack on her desk. As soon as he stepped into the room, she straightened, pushed those adorable glasses up her pert nose and smiled at him. Professionally.

Hell, he was fighting to hide the most painful erection he'd ever experienced and Rachel was standing in front of him in a damn flowered dress that went all the way up to her freaking neck. The thing even had a lace collar! But now he knew that she wore garters! And silk stockings!

His eyes darted to her chest, then back up to her eyes. Was she wearing a sexy bra too? Would it match the black lace garter?

Oh hell, his erection throbbed now and he had to lean over her desk in order to not scare her.

"Good morning. Thank you for coming back to Izara to help with this project." White socks, he thought frantically. She probably wore white socks and sweatpants to sleep in. And curlers. Yeah, he could picture her in curlers. Maybe the curlers were why her gorgeous, auburn hair curled like that.

Nope, that wasn't working. The white socks were fine, but then his eyes moved over her figure as she searched for a file and all he could do was picture her in the white socks and...nothing else.

Ah hell!

"On the flight last night, I read through the information you sent me. I'm eager to get started. I had some thoughts and..." she looked up and must have seen the pain on his face. Pulling back, she folded her hands. "I'm sorry, Your Highness. I'm sure that you have this covered already. I shouldn't presume to have any additional information."

He laughed softly. "Rachel, your ideas are exactly why I thought you would be an excellent addition to this project. So please, don't worry about me. I got slammed onto the mat by Gaelen this morning." He stood up, back in control. Barely. "How about if we go into my office and discuss the project? I'd love to hear your ideas." Also, his desk might help hide his inevitable erection!

Her smile brightened and Tarin was once again reminded of how lovely she was. Rachel wasn't the glamorous type who wore long, dark lashes and red lipstick. She didn't wear a size double D bra or teeter around on five inch heels.

Just the opposite and, for some reason, the combination of her perfect, pale skin, soft lashes, pink-tinged, wide mouth and those cute glasses just...did it for him. Her hair was an auburn brown, but had the most intriguing red highlights. He knew because he'd sat behind her during a conference last year and watched the overhead lights shimmer in her tresses.

He looked down at her fingers with the clean, tapered fingernails and no rings, and thought about wrapping his fingers around her wrist. She was so slight, he could circle her wrist with his thumb and forefinger and have room to spare.

Meanwhile, he was a huge hulk of a man who knew how to build things and tear them down. With a sigh, he moved into his office, thinking that they were the perfect example of opposites attracting.

Except that she hadn't ever shown even the slightest bit of interest in him. In fact, she barely even seemed to know he was alive while she'd worked for Talia. She never looked at him, always moved out of his way when they met the hallway and, even when he'd tried to smile in her direction, she was so busy and focused that she never noticed.

She followed him into his office, perching on the edge of the leather chair in front of his desk.

"Okay so what's on your mind?" he asked.

She flipped the page on her notebook. "You have a meeting in four minutes with..." and she started to list his agenda for the day. Tarin leaned back, enjoying the soft, lilting southern accent in her voice. It wasn't thick, like some people he'd heard. Instead, it was subtle. It was things like "ay" instead of "I" or just an additional syllable in some words.

She sat there, looking at him expectantly, and he realized that he needed to say something.

"Your meeting, Your Highness?" she offered.

He leaned his arms on the desk in front of him. "We need to get something straight first."

Rachel immediately lifted her pen, her eyes riveted to him as she eagerly awaited his instructions. "Yes?"

"My name is Tarin. You are never to refer to me as Your Highness, is that understood?"

She pulled back and he wanted to laugh at her indignant expression. "I don't think that's appropriate, Your Highness."

He laughed softly. "Isn't it my call?"

She pressed her lips together, the perfect picture of a disapproving librarian. A sexy, disapproving librarian. One that hid garters and silk stockings underneath a demure flowered dress!

Rachel glanced pointedly at her watch. "Shouldn't you be in your meeting now?" she repeated, a reprimand in her tone.

He chuckled again. "Fine. We'll talk about it later. But Rachel?" he prompted, standing up and waiting until she was standing as well, looking up at him with those huge, green eyes that were barely tempered by the severe glasses.

"Yes, Your Highness?"

His grin widened. "I *always* win," and then he walked out of his office, heading towards his first meeting of the day. "Are you coming?" he called over his shoulder.

He felt her jump at his bark, smiling as he glanced over his shoulder towards her.

"Coming?" she parroted, startled.

"Yes. This meeting is the first discussion about the university project. I need your feedback and you need to hear what's going on right from the start."

With huge eyes, she jerked forward, stumbling slightly. He caught her arm and they both froze. He looked down into her eyes and wanted to lose himself in those emerald depths.

Before he could do something stupid though, he pulled away and nodded towards the opposite door. "This way," he replied, his voice gruffer than he'd intended.

They walked into the meeting and sat down. He noticed that Rachel took one of the chairs along the wall, even though there were several empty chairs at the conference table. He didn't understand why, but let her sit where she was comfortable.

Rachel smiled as she walked down the hallway later that afternoon. She felt as if she was tingling with happiness and challenge! And excitement. She couldn't ignore the excitement she felt just being near Tarin again.

He was so amazing! She'd watched him in several meetings today, encouraging everyone to talk, never shooting down an idea, no matter how ill conceived. Rachel didn't think he'd care about her opinions on the ideas being tossed around. She knew that her job was to facilitate everyone else's ideas. Hence why she was walking back to her office now to organize a long travel plan. Tarin wanted to interview several leading architects, needing to feel them out and get a sense of who they were.

An hour later, she'd called the palace travel office and given them Prince Tarin's itinerary, organized hotels in each of the cities, and coordinated with his housekeeping staff and security team.

It was after hours now and she guessed that Tarin had gone to eat dinner with his family. She knew that they enjoyed meals together, especially since they all seemed to take a hand in raising the two orphaned nieces, Elsa and Ellora. Those two darlings were getting on in school now and were normal, rambunctious young ladies. Amit was the closest to a father figure that the girls had, but Gaelen and Tarin both made themselves available for advice or conversations, or especially fun activities.

It was one of the things she loved about this family. They were just that: a family. There were no harsh insults, no passive aggressive compliments, and no power grabs, which she knew happened in other royal families. Furthermore, there was no ridicule for dressing one way or another, no competition for grades or friends or girlfriends.

Unlike in her family, she thought with a groan.

Not that Rachel and her older sister, Wendy, ever competed for anything. What a ridiculous thought. As if Rachel could even compete with Wendy's beauty and glamor.

Packing up, she glanced around to ensure that everything was neat and tidy, then headed home...or at least, back to the temporary apartment she'd be calling home while working on this project.

Chapter 3

Tarin tapped his pen against his notebook, bored out of his mind. Rachel wasn't cleared for military briefings, so she wasn't with him. It was just him, Gaelen, and Amit, as well as Izara's generals and he wanted to toss these papers aside and get the hell out of here.

Amit and Gaelen seemed to be enraptured by the newest information on troop movements, readiness capabilities, and the seemingly endless issues with their enemies...and their allies. There really was no such thing as a trustworthy ally in the game of world politics. Friendships were formed out of necessity and loyalty, but both could be shattered with one false move.

Rachel would give her loyalty and friendship completely, he thought. More tapping. More fidgeting in his chair.

"Are we boring you with this national security stuff?" Amit demanded, turning away from the generals to glare at Tarin.

Tarin laughed. "Nah. I'm utterly fascinated." He turned to the general. "Please proceed. I'm completely enraptured."

The generals shared in the laugh, knowing that their information was dry. "I think we're about finished for now," he replied.

Even Gaelen smiled, although he tried to appear stern while in Amit's presence. Chronologically, their oldest brother might be only a few years older, but Amit was an old man at heart. He loved spending time with his family, had never really gone out and sowed his wild oats. He was a home body who worked intensely during the day, only to escape to his family's private quarters to play with his small kids, then pick up his sketch pads or paintbrush and free his mind as he captured his children or wife's smiles on paper and canvas.

Slowly, everyone stood up from the conference room table, but Tarin was aware that no one seemed to be in a hurry to leave. So, instead

17

of sprinting out the door in order to go find Rachel, he waited around, chatting and joking with the others.

"I have to get back to work," he finally muttered to someone, he wasn't really sure who. With that announcement, he turned and walked out, eager to see Rachel's huge, green eyes and quirky smile. Yeah, he had it bad, he thought as he headed down the long hallway.

Rachel watched the instructional video carefully. She nodded along, shifting in small half movements, locking the next steps into her memory.

"Right!" she muttered, then stepped into position. Arms up. Chin up. "And...one, two, three, four. One, two, three, four." Her mind focused on keeping her left elbow high, her right arm straight and tight. "No spaghetti arms!" she reminded herself. "One, two, three, four. One, two, three, four."

The music swelled from her computer and she glanced over her shoulder at the video that was playing. "And turn!" the man in the video called out.

"Turn?" she muttered, glaring over her shoulder at the laptop. "Turn how? And where am I supposed to turn?"

"Definitely avoid the other people," a deep voice offered from the doorway. "And avoid the furniture too."

Rachel jumped about a foot in the air and swung around, finding Tarin leaning in the doorway.

For a long moment, Rachel stood there, her hand to her heart as she looked at the enormous man lounging in the doorway. Finally, she pulled herself together. "How long have you been standing there?" she demanded, struggling to regain her balance, and folding her hands nervously in front of her. The music on the video increased and the man called out, "Remember your...!" He didn't get a chance to finish since Rachel slapped her laptop closed. She struggled to appear professional even though she knew that Tarin had probably heard and seen everything. Good grief!

"Long enough," he replied and pushed away from the doorway to step into her office. "Are you learning how to dance?"

"Yes. I just..."

"From a video?"

Rachel sighed, her shoulders drooping slightly. But she rallied quickly, pulling herself back and looking Tarin straight in the eye! "Yes. I try to improve myself in various ways and...well, dancing is something I've always wanted to learn."

"Did you ever take dance classes when you were a kid?" he asked, moving closer.

From this distance, he was so close, she could see the golden flecks in his hazel eyes. Fascinating!

"Rachel?" he prompted.

Rachel jerked slightly, pulling her eyes away from his. "Um…yes. I begged my mother to let me take ballet lessons." She smiled crookedly, lifting one shoulder. "She finally signed me up for classes but…apparently, she thought I was too klutzy and looked ridiculous trying the various steps, so my mother only allowed me to take a few classes."

Tarin cocked a dark brow. "Klutzy? I doubt it."

She grimaced. "I don't see how you can. I'm always tripping over things." Only when you're around, she finished mentally.

He shrugged a shoulder, dismissing her assertion. "I bet you're a beautiful dancer, Rachel," he said, his voice dropping just enough to make her shiver.

She looked up at him, saw the soft look in his eyes and something melted inside of her. "Yes. Well, dancing has always been a dream of mine. But…," she licked her lips, thinking she should move back, put some space between their bodies. Instead, she stood still, transfixed. "I'll figure it out." She turned and picked up a file folder from a stack on her desk. "Here are the proposals you asked for. Plus, I did a bit of research and added a couple more architectural firms that you might want to consider. I evaluated your criteria from the previous list and compared that criteria to some other firms. Any that matched, I pulled up information for your review and included details in this file," she explained, handing him another file. "I hope you don't mind."

He flipped open the second file and skimmed through the pages. "This is great work, Rachel. Thank you for doing this."

"You have another meeting with the Water Board in five minutes," she explained.

He sighed, closing the file folder. "Right. Back to the boring stuff, huh?"

She tried to hide her smile, but he was just so irreverent! "I guess so, Your…" Rachel stopped when she saw the warning in his hazel gaze. Shifting her feet, she glared up at him, although she was unaware of her expression. "I can't call you by you first name," she declared. "It's disrespectful and inappropriate."

He grinned. "Ah, but don't you love living on the wild side?" He put the files down on her desk, then leaned his fists against it. "Come on. Try it. I dare you! Say my name, just once. I bet it would feel liberating!"

Rachel rolled her eyes, fighting back a laugh at his teasing. Carefully, she folded her hands in front of her. "You're going to get me fired."

He laughed. "No way. You're too valuable. I can't fire you."

Her lips quirked slightly, but she quickly shook her head, unaware of the prim, librarian-like way she was standing. Pushing her glasses higher onto her nose, she shook her head. "I'm not using your first name," she told him firmly.

His eyes sparkled with mischief. "I'll fire you if you don't," he returned.

She rolled her eyes, adding a bit of a huff for emphasis. "You just said I was too valuable to fire. Now, you're threatening to fire me if I don't follow your completely inappropriate order?"

Another shrug of that deliciously muscular shoulder and she had to press her lips together to stop herself from laughing out loud.

"I'm fickle. So sue me. But you'll have to use my first name in court."

She crossed her arms over her stomach. "Your Highness, has anyone ever told you that you're a horrible man?"

He chuckled, straightened to his full height and grabbed the files again. "All the time." He turned around. "I'll be in this meeting for about an hour. Would you mind sticking around so that we can discuss these firms over dinner tonight?"

"Absolutely!" she replied. Then, just because she was in a good mood, she added, "Your Highness."

He'd already disappeared through the doorway, but he'd obviously heard her because he stuck his head back through the door. "You're going to pay for that," he warned.

At her laughter, he once again disappeared, and Rachel slapped her hand over her mouth, trying to hide her amusement. "Good grief," she grumbled happily. "That man is..." she didn't finish the sentence because too many "wrong" adjectives popped into her head. Describing Prince Tarin as horrible, sexy, gorgeous, or anything else was a bad move professionally.

Sitting down at her desk, she re-opened her laptop, still smiling at the short interchange with Prince Tarin. Working for Tarin was definitely different than working for Talia. The princess was kinder, asking for assistance and offering praise constantly. Rachel felt like a dynamo while in her employ.

Tarin was far more demanding, she thought. He didn't ask, he ordered. But for some reason, she sort of liked that. She liked his autocratic demeanor. Maybe because...her head tilted slightly as she contemplated the differences in Tarin and Talia's work methods. For the life of her, she couldn't seem to figure out why she liked Tarin's managerial style slightly better.

But she definitely understood why she liked his eyes! Rachel sighed wistfully, thinking about those teasing, hazel eyes of his. She loved the way he looked at her, as if he truly saw *her* and not just the overly efficient, prim, future-owner-of-twenty-cats lady.

No, the way he looked at her wasn't the kind of look a man gave to a woman. It was just...sort of flattering in a strange, breathtaking way. Rachel was pretty sure that Tarin didn't have any idea that his attention caused her body to crave unspoken things. He couldn't ever know that her breasts tingled with awareness whenever he walked into a room. Good grief, that would be humiliating!

Pushing her completely irrelevant reactions to the man's presence aside, she focused on work. Unfortunately, the project demands hadn't really kicked in yet, so there wasn't much to work through at this point. She suspected that she'd be swamped in a week or so, but right now, everything was slow.

"Great," she muttered, slumping slightly over her desk and looking around for something more to accomplish. "Can't go home, but why would I? Not much to do there either." She leaned back in her chair and adjusted the folds of her flowered skirt more primly over her knees. "It isn't even my home," she grumbled, thinking about the luxurious apartment that the Izara government had allowed her to use for the duration of this project. But it wasn't her home. She didn't feel comfortable rearranging the furniture or hanging her pictures or...doing anything. Good grief, she even felt weird sleeping in the bed because it wasn't made up with her personal sheets!

"I'm weird," she sighed.

Chapter 4

"Come with me," Tarin ordered, stepping into Rachel's office and look-ing down at her startled face.

"What's wrong?"

He couldn't stop the frown as he took in her silk blouse and the pleat-ed, navy skirt. He didn't like the outfit. Not even a little! He preferred Rachel in the flowered things she normally wore. The flowered dresses and skirt just seemed...right on her.

Ignoring his irritation over her outfit, he shook his head. "Nothing. This way," he urged as she circled her desk to follow.

"Where are we going?" she asked.

He slowed when he realized that she was almost running to keep up with him. He had to remind himself how tiny she was. "How tall are you?" he asked, turning right, heading towards the area of the palace where the more formal entertainments happened.

"I'm tall enough," she snapped.

He laughed, shaking his head. "Seriously. Five six? Five five?"

Tarin watched her bristle with irritation, but she admitted, "I'm five feet, four inches tall. Which is tall enough for anything that I need to do."

He laughed, thinking her umbrage was adorable in a sex-kitten sort of way. "Well, at six foot, four and a half, you're teeny to me."

She glared up at him. "I don't see how my height is relevant to my employment."

"It isn't relevant to your employment. I just wanted to know," he said, stopping in front of a set of double doors. "But at the moment, I'm going to teach you to dance, so I assure you, it's relevant." He pushed open the doors to reveal the palace ballroom.

Normally, there would be hundreds of guests milling around this room, networking and being seen. The lights would be brightly lit and there would be an orchestra set up in one corner. The ballroom could hold anywhere between five hundred and a thousand guests with enough space for mingling while tuxedo clad wait staff walked around with drinks and appetizers.

At the moment though, the room was empty and mostly dark. He flipped a few switches and soft lights came on, creating a more romantic effect than he'd anticipated, but appreciated.

"Dance?" she squeaked.

He ignored her stunned protest and walked over to the stereo system controls. He fiddled with a few of the dials and, a moment later, soft music flowed through the room. He looked up, listened for a moment, and nodded with approval.

"This will work," he said, then turned to find Rachel watching him with huge, worried eyes.

"Come here," he said reaching for her. "One hand on my shoulder and," he took her other hand in his, feeling her trembling as he put his hand on her waist. "Just follow my lead," he whispered.

With slow, deliberate movements, he led her through the steps of the foxtrot, not taking large steps, but enough so that she could learn the rhythm of the dance. "This is the basic step," he told her. "Just form a square in your mind and let your feet follow."

She stared at his chest, not daring to look him in the eye when they were so close. That was okay...for now. Soon though, he wanted her looking up at him when they danced.

"I...this feels awkward."

He tightened his grip on her hand, warning her that he was going to turn slightly. "Why is that?" Tarin smiled with appreciation when she easily followed his lead. She was a natural!

"Because you're my boss."

He turned again and she deftly swiveled along with him. "Actually, Talia is your boss. You're just helping me on a specific project." He shifted again. "Relax and enjoy the music, Rachel."

She took a deep breath, staring at his chest as she concentrated. "One, two, three, four," she whispered.

"Stop counting," he instructed gently. "Just feel the music. Feel my hands leading you through the steps."

She smiled slightly, and stopped counting. As soon as she did that, the rhythm seemed to infect her legs and feet. She smiled up at him, her eyes bright with excitement and wonder.

"See?" he prompted, feeling her muscles relax. Even the nervous trembling seemed to subside.

"How did you learn to dance?" she asked.

He shifted so that they were dancing in a circle. He doubted that she even noticed.

"It's required of all members of any royal family. We also need to know how to ride horses as expertly as any jockey, speak several languages and know how to charm leaders of the various countries."

Her shoulders seemed to melt. "Oh, I'd love to learn to ride," she sighed.

The more she relaxed, the more easily her body flowed with the music. "You're an excellent dancer, once you let yourself enjoy it."

She blushed and he thought she was absolutely enchanting. "You're a good teacher."

"No, there's more to it than that. You have to have innate abilities in order to dance. There's a rhythm to the music. But if a person doesn't feel it in their soul, then they'll never *really* learn to dance. Some people can do all of the steps to a dance," he continued, spinning her, his feet moving between her legs and she automatically placed her feet between his, perfectly following his lead. "But they'll never truly enjoy the beauty of dancing. Music and dancing comes from the soul, not the mind. You have to *feel* the dance."

She stared at his chest, but he could feel her body, felt the sensations flowing through her. Tarin had learned to dance at an early age, under protest, but as he'd grown older, he'd learned to enjoy it. It was a good way to get to know the ladies and a perfect opportunity to avoid irritating conversations. When an annoying diplomat approached, one he didn't want to talk to, he simply asked the wife to dance.

Dancing with Rachel was different. It wasn't just moving to the music together, he realized. They were...*dancing*! He could feel her body, feel the music flowing through her. When her fingers tightened on his shoulder, he pulled her closer.

"It's polite to look at your partner when dancing," he said, his voice sounding deeper as his body reacted.

She looked up at him, tilting her head backwards.

"That's better," he muttered, his fingers tightening around her hand. Tarin refrained from pulling her flush against his body, even though everything inside of him clamored for him to do so. But if he did, she'd feel his reaction, notice his arousal. He didn't want to scare her away even if dancing with her was the most erotic foreplay he'd ever experienced.

"You're a wonderful dancer," she whispered, her lips barely moving as those huge eyes of hers stared up at him.

"You're a wonderful student," he replied and swung her around. "Are you ready for the next step?"

She grinned crookedly and his heart thudded. "I doubt it."

He laughed. "We're going for it anyway. Just follow my lead." He stepped back, one hand still on her waist and, with his fingers, guided her under his arm, twirling her around and then stepping back just in time for her to move elegantly and smoothly back into his arms.

"Perfect," he murmured.

Her eyes widened and he saw the glow in her eyes. Excitement? Arousal?

Tarin mentally groaned as he pushed that thought away. "Are you hungry?" he asked instead.

Rachel felt as if she were floating on air. There was no hardwood floor beneath her. The lights were actually stars and Prince Tarin was her lover, carefully spinning a sensual web around her as the music played in the background.

"Hungry?" she asked, wanting to giggle. But she never giggled. She used to giggle, but then...nope. No more giggling. She'd stopped her-self from doing it because it was embarrassing.

"Dinner. Are you hungry for dinner?"

Rachel stared up at him, somehow sensing that food wasn't really what was on his mind. But if not food, what would he be thinking about? Of course it was food! She was Rachel, so food was the only thing he was talking about.

Carefully stepping out of his arms, she folded her hands in front of her, as was her habit. "If you want to discuss the options of the other architectural firms, I can just..."

He took her hand, pulling her towards the stereo system. With a flip of his fingers, the music died. "You're having dinner," he countered. "I doubt you've had time to get to the grocery store since you flew into Izara the other night. And you were here at the palace too early this morning. From now on, we don't start working until at least eight o'clock in the morning," he told her with a warning glance. "No sneak-ing in at seven. Got it?"

"Yes, sir," she laughed, then slapped a hand over her mouth. "Sorry. That was unprofessional."

He grinned and put a hand to the small of her back, leading her out of the ballroom. "You have a nice laugh, Rachel. I'd like to hear it more often."

Her shoulders curled inward slightly and she shot a quick glance up at him, then away. "I don't. Not really. I know it's annoying."

He looked down at her, startled. She could feel his surprise. "Why do you think that you have an annoying laugh?"

She shrugged, deciding that a change of subject was necessary. "The architects that I found are a bit smaller in size than the ones that you originally chose," she said, walking alongside him. "But a few of them have truly innovative ideas that are both more energy efficient and faster, using less resources while implementing building techniques that last longer and with lower maintenance costs."

"That sounds interesting," he replied as they entered a small dining room with a table set for two. "But you didn't answer my question. Who told you that you have an annoying laugh?"

Drat the man! Did he have to be so tenacious? Couldn't he just let an uncomfortable subject drop?

No, Rachel accepted. Tarin didn't like unsolved mysteries.

Draping the napkin over her lap, she felt...tight. Her shoulders were tense and every muscle in her body rebelled at the thought of admitting this to him. But she couldn't lie or dismiss the issue. So honesty was what she gave him.

Looking down, she shrugged her shoulders ever so slightly. "My family prides itself on being very honest with each other, Your Highness," she explained carefully. "So, back to these architects..."

Tarin understood exactly what she was doing and he debated whether to allow her to change the subject. Personally, he thought her laugh was sexy as hell. So maybe he should let her go on believing that she shouldn't laugh.

Perhaps for the moment, he'd let her get away with the change of subject, but circle back to the issue of her laughter at a later time.

"Fine. Tell me about their innovative building ideas."

He watched as her eyes lit up, banishing the pain he'd seen moments before. Whatever she was about to say, it was something she was truly passionate about. Leaning forward, he was fascinated by the change in her.

"Well, I've been reading about alternative building materials. Traditional steel and concrete are fine, obviously, but there are so many other building options available! And since you're planning to build an entire university center, wouldn't it be a good idea to try some of these innovations? Test them and see if the students can improve upon them? I mean, just imagine it! This university could become a center for innovation and experimentation in the science and technology industry!"

He smiled, thinking once again how beautiful she was. Her huge eyes and that quirky smile that curled higher on one side when she smiled made her look gamin and fairy-like. When she wasn't smiling, Rachel was delicate and elegant. But when she smiled…damn, she was stunning! Plus, her auburn curls literally vibrated with the energy she barely managed to contain in such a petite package.

"Tell me more," he said, waving to the serving staff who immediately brought in the first course.

"Have you ever heard of nanocrystals?" she asked. He had, but he didn't react, allowing her to explain them. "These crystals allow light to filter in, just like regular glass, but they block out all heat, making windows much more efficient! Just think about how much that could reduce cooling costs here in Izara, where the afternoon temperatures get up to a million degrees."

He laughed at her hyperbole, waving his fork towards her plate. "Eat while you talk," he ordered.

She stabbed a piece of chicken. "There are also wool and seaweed bricks. These materials allow…" she stopped and grimaced. "Okay, those are more effective in cold climates," she continued, tilting her head to the side as another thought occurred to her. "There is also something called synthetic spider silk. It's stronger than steel by a huge measure, but can make acoustic building tiles and other spaces." She stopped and frowned thoughtfully. "I don't know if it is lighter though. So, I'm not sure if it would be useful here. Nor am I aware of how it would hold up in dust storms."

She shrugged and stuffed the bite of chicken into her mouth.

Over the course of the meal, they debated various building materials, their benefits and uses in a hot climate, where the temperatures could rise and fall over seventy degrees on a daily basis. The afternoons in the summer months were normally in the triple digits while the night-time temperatures dipped into the fifties and sixties, cool enough to warrant a sweater.

The whole time, he watched her face, fascinated by the changes. When she concentrated, her full lips pressed together. When he countered her idea with one of his own, her lips softened as she absorbed and processed the new information, comparing that data to what she already knew. Her eyes were huge and she took off her glasses, setting them to the side, which made the green of her irises almost glow with excitement.

As the waiters took the empty dessert plates away, Rachel was startled by how much she'd eaten, but also at how comfortable she felt in Tarin's presence.

"You're not as scary as everyone thinks you are," she teased, standing up and placing the linen napkin on her chair.

"Oh, I'm very scary," he replied, standing as well. "Never doubt it. I'm one of the scariest of my brothers."

She laughed, then quickly pressed her lips together. "No, that title goes to Sheik el Raminar. Now that is one scary man!"

"Eh, he's a pussycat," he countered, putting a hand to the small of her back. "Come, I'll take you back to your apartment."

She pulled back, jumping slightly from the heat coming from the touch of his hand. Before, his touch had felt comforting in an oddly tingly way. But now, maybe because of the half a glass of wine she'd consumed during the meal, she felt...alive! Alive and alert and...much more tingly than before dinner.

"You don't have to see me home, Your..." she stopped at the warning in his eyes. But instead of saying his name, she pressed her lips together, fighting back a smile. Finally, she said, "I can walk home. The apartment is just around the corner."

"Nonsense. It's late at night. I'll walk you home."

Walk her home? Prince Tarin? Out in the open? "You can't!" she gasped.

"Why not?"

"Because you're a member of the royal family. You can't go out in the streets unprotected."

He laughed softly. "Yes, I can. I do it all the time."

She rolled her eyes. "No, you don't. You have a herd of personal guards surrounding you at all times," she gestured to the two men standing just outside the dining room. "Right there." She moved a foot away from him. "I promise, I'll be safe. It's just a short walk."

"If you won't let me walk you home, then one of the palace guards will accompany you," he told her. "Either that, or you're staying here inside the palace."

She almost choked at the idea of staying here. "I definitely can't stay here!" she told him. "That would be...!"

He shook his head, lifting his hand to stop her argument. "Actually, that makes a whole lot more sense. I think you should just stay here."

What was he suggesting?! Stay? In the palace? Good grief, that would be a massive breach in protocol! "No!"

He laughed. "Rachel, are you seriously disobeying a direct order?"

Rachel stopped her next horrified objection, her mouth hanging open for one embarrassing moment. When she realized that she truly was arguing with him, her mouth snapped shut but she glared at him. "No, of course I wouldn't do that. But..."

"Good. Then it's settled."

"No. I won't stay here. It isn't appropriate. I'm an employee of the Izara government. You've already given me a lovely apartment, Your..."

she stopped just in time. Her lips curved upwards, but she wouldn't let her laughter out. "I'm fine where I am. And if it will make you feel better, I'll get a cab to drive me the two blocks to my apartment."

And with that, she turned on her heel and walked out of the dining room. "Good night, Your Highness," she called over her shoulder. "And thank you for a wonderful evening." She even added a bit of a curtsy, feeling outrageously daring at the moment. Then hurried out, her navy skirt flapping against her knees as she rushed down the hallway before he could stop her.

Tarin watched her hurry away, wondering if she really thought she could escape him so easily. All he had to do was make a quick phone call and she'd be stopped by any number of the guards. So her hurried pace wasn't going to save her. Hell, he could walk and catch up with her, since her legs were so much shorter than his. He almost laughed out loud at her belief that she'd won this round.

And why the hell wouldn't she use his first name? As he watched her peek over her shoulder at him, he suspected it had become a game to her. A game he was determined to win, he thought with increasing relish.

Thinking of her reactions while they were dancing, his mind moved in a different direction, contemplating the pros and cons of what he wanted, versus what might be best. When he realized that both of those answers were the same, he smiled with triumph. Yes, my beautiful Rachel. You are going to be mine, he decided.

Chapter 5

Rachel blinked at the text message, not sure that she was awake enough to understand. "What does he mean? Paris?"

Leaning back against the pillows, she took several deep breaths and re-read the message. "Paris? He wants to fly off to Paris?" For a long moment, she tried to remember the list of cities that he'd mentioned yesterday. She'd spoken to the travel office and...thinking hard...nope, Paris had not been on that list.

The loud knock on her door startled her and she looked around, wondering who would be knocking so early in the morning.

"Just a minute!" she called out. "Probably the property manager again," she grumbled, grabbing her favorite silk robe. Her hair probably looked like a tumbleweed and her face was clean of makeup. She wore only the small cami and her panties that she'd slept in, but the silk robe covered enough of her sleep attire that she felt comfortable opening the door.

Tying the belt of her robe around her waist, she padded over to the entrance, paused to take a deep breath, then pulled it open. "Good morn...."

Rachel stopped and stared as she found Prince Tarin standing in her doorway. Was he rumpled and sleepy like her? Nope, of course not! He stood there looking fresh, alive, and magnetic in a dark suit and blue tie, freshly shaven and smelling like something clean and spicy.

"Your Highness!" she gasped, grabbing the collar of her robe and holding it tightly closed.

He pressed the door wider and stepped into the room, forcing Rachel to step back to make space for him.

"What are you doing here?" she demanded, tucking her hair back behind her ear in the hopes that it wasn't as messy as she suspected.

"Is that how you normally answer the door?" he demanded, eyeing her silk robe pointedly.

Rachel glanced down and hissed when she realized her nipples were pressing against the silk. She crossed her arms protectively and frowned up at Tarin. "No. Usually, the people who knock on my door don't do it this early in the morning. So normally I'm showered and dressed in appropriate clothes."

Instead of apologizing, he grunted. As if that meant something to her? She had no clue what a grunt meant. She didn't speak caveman. So she rolled her eyes and demanded, "Is there a reason why you are at my door this early?"

He smiled. "Not a morning person, are you?"

She pressed her lips together, not sure what to say. "I am normally at the office very early each day. If you ever have an issue with my...?"

"No! My apologies. I didn't mean to imply any such thing," he countered and moved closer.

Just a step, but it was a significant step because now she could smell his aftershave and her heart pounded violently against her ribs. Darn it, she needed to put some space between them, but she'd backed herself into a corner with the sofa behind her.

"So...why are you here, Your Highness?"

He frowned. "Didn't we just have a conversation yesterday about you calling me Tarin?"

She shrugged, fighting to control her trembling. "Yes, I believe we did have that conversation."

"And?"

Rachel refused to be intimidated. If she was going to work with him over the next several months, she needed to show him that she wouldn't be intimidated. "And I disagreed," she told him tartly, pretending as if she weren't standing in front of him in only a silk robe and not much else.

His lips curled up slightly but he didn't argue her point. "Ah, Rachel, I think we're going to get along just fine."

That was such a startling claim, she blinked, taken aback. "We are?"

He nodded and she vaguely wondered how he got such a close shave. By late afternoon, he looked all sexy and scruffy. But right now, he looked...gorgeous!

"We are. And today, we're flying to Paris. How soon can you be ready to go?"

"Paris?" she echoed, not sure she'd heard him correctly.

"Yes. Paris."

Rachel looked around, her arms dropping unconsciously. "I can't go to

Paris!"

"Why not?"

"Because...," she huffed, trying to force her brain to start working. But she hadn't had coffee yet. She really needed coffee! Rachel fully admitted that she probably drank more coffee than was good for her, but she didn't care. Working in a high pressure environment such as with Princess Talia and, now, with Prince Tarin, coffee was her friend! So she relied on vague emphatic replies. "I can't just fly off to Paris!" she said.

"Do you have a cat?"

A cat? "No." What an odd question.

"A dog?" He pressed.

Irritated now, Rachel shook her head. "No!"

"A passport?"

"No!" She shook her head, then she realized what he'd asked and closed her eyes with irritation. "I mean...yes! But...!"

"A boyfriend?" He had the audacity to peer into the bedroom.

Automatically, she stepped in front of the door, afraid he might see the rumpled sheets and think...well, she had no idea what he might think. Coffee! She really needed coffee! "No!"

His hands clapped together, then he rubbed them together. "Excellent. Then jump in the shower and pack a bag. I'll make coffee while you shower."

Rachel's eyes narrowed. "Your Highness, do you even *know* how to make coffee?"

He laughed and shrugged one of those deliciously massive shoulders. "I never have before, but how hard can it be?"

Oh, the joyful mysteries of the coffee maker! This should be fun! "Okay, sounds good. I'll get ready and pack. You make coffee and I'll be ready in about twenty minutes, if that's okay with your schedule?"

He looked towards her bedroom again, almost as if he were trying to figure out how to cut that twenty minutes down into ten. "Fine. Twenty minutes." Then he turned to face the kitchen.

Rachel stared at his back for a long moment and shook her head as she padded towards the bedroom. "I wish I had a camera for this," and she disappeared into the bedroom, closing the door, then hurrying to the shower.

Tarin eyed the kitchen countertops, not sure which machine was the coffee maker. Sure he had coffee every morning, but his coffee appeared on the table or was rolled into his apartment on a tray, already made. Usually even poured for him since the palace staff knew exactly how he preferred his coffee.

He heard the shower start and groaned, his attention straying from his coffee-making task. She was naked, he thought. Naked and wet and running her soft, delicate hands all over her body!

Tarin leaned against the edge of the counter, willing himself to focus on his task...which was what? Walking into the shower so that he could join her? Watch her hands slide over her dewy skin? Nibble her taut, wet nipples as...!

"This was a bad plan," he sighed. Shaking himself, he returned his attention to the coffee maker dilemma. There were several appliances lined up neatly along the counter, pressed back against the wall. But which was the coffee maker?

The one with the coffee-pot-looking-thing underneath! Triumphantly, he pulled it out and stared at it. "Okay, you've identified the machine, now what?"

Coffee! Yep, a coffee maker needed coffee, right? Or did it have the coffee already in it?

Opening and closing the various parts of the coffee maker, he discovered there was no coffee in it. It also occurred to him that he wasn't exactly sure what coffee looked like before it was brewed. He knew that coffee was essentially boiled beans but...where were the beans? Where did the beans go in the coffee maker?

He searched through the cabinets and spotted the bag labeled "coffee grounds", which he opened. That smelled good, he thought with a nod. He even spotted a coffee maker manual and grinned. Flipping through the pages, he rolled his eyes at the warnings, finally coming to the page with the instructions.

"Filter? Why the hell does the coffee maker need a filter?"

A small chuckle behind him warned Tarin that he was no longer alone.

Turning, he spotted her over his shoulder and swallowed a groan. She wore another one of those flowery dresses, this one had a round neck and the extra visible skin drew his eyes. She had the palest, most delicate skin he'd ever seen! Plus, it was dewy from her recent shower. Her hair was twisted up into a towel and she wore no makeup. Tarin had seen his past mistresses done up with their hair like that, but none had looked as sexy as Rachel. He had no idea why, but seeing her like this, with her long neck exposed, his body reacted...predictably.

"Need some help?" she asked innocently, laughter dancing in her eyes.

Pulling his gaze away from her, he stared blankly at the coffee machine manual, unable to read the words, but it was better than staring at her. And wondering what kind of underwear she was wearing under that hideous dress. He shook his head, trying to clear away the thought. "No. Go away. I'll have the coffee ready in a minute."

She shifted, tying something behind her. Involuntarily, he turned to watch. This dress was navy blue with big, white tulips all over it. It wrapped around her, cinching tightly around her tiny waist, and show-casing how round and lush her hips were. She didn't have large breasts, but what she had were perfect. Not too small, not too big. Just perfect. For a long moment, he stared, his mouth watering as he pictured those breasts bare and heaving. Pictured himself touching those breasts and taking them into his...!

"Your Highness?" she asked.

Brutally, he ripped his gaze from her breasts and looked into those amazing green eyes of hers. She wasn't wearing her glasses at the moment, so he could see her eyes clearly. They looked confused and thankfully, not offended by his lack of discipline.

"Right. Go away. I'm making coffee and it's going to be good." He looked down at the manual again, trying to read the words but all he could see were her breasts.

"If you let me, I can have the coffee brewing in just a...."

"I'm on it," he said firmly, not bothering to look up.

"Fine," she replied and he heard the soft chuckle. He also thought he heard something along the lines of, "I can get it at the corner store faster than this." She disappeared back into the bathroom before he could demand that she repeat her comment.

Staring blankly at the instruction manual, he sighed with irritation. A moment later, he tossed the manual back into the cabinet and stormed to the front door. His guards stood in the hallway, alert and tense. "Do either of you know how to make coffee?" he asked.

Both of them blinked at him, confused. "Your Highness?" one of them asked, needing clarification.

"Coffee," he repeated. "I told Rachel I'd make coffee for her, but I can't figure out the coffee machine. Either of you know how?"

They shared a bemused glance before one stepped forward slightly. "Come on. I have to hurry before she finishes."

He heard the hair dryer turn on as the guard followed him into the apartment. He walked over to the coffee machine, eyed the machine, and nodded. "This has a reusable filter, Your Highness. You just add coffee grounds in here, and water in here, then press this button."

The man efficiently scooped several spoonfuls of coffee grounds into the machine, filled up the carafe with water, then poured it carefully into the reservoir, slid the carafe into the machine and pressed the but-ton. "That's it, Your Highness."

He nodded, absorbing the knowledge for the future. "Excellent. Thank you."

"Anytime, Your Highness," the guard said, and returned to his post outside. Tarin spotted the man's smile at his inabilities, but, thankfully, the man didn't say anything. He simply pulled the apartment door closed, leaving Tarin to search for mugs.

He was sitting down on the sofa with a cup of perfectly brewed coffee, flipping through a magazine when she emerged. He almost laughed at her skeptical expression.

Silently, he took a sip of the coffee.

"How did you…?" she asked, then stopped, looking over at the coffee maker. There was another cup set beside the coffee, so she carefully poured a cup. Taking a sip, she sighed happily and nodded her head. "Okay, you did it." She took another sip, eyeing him over the rim of the cup. "*How* did you do it?"

"Are you questioning my masculinity by assuming I can't figure out how to make coffee?"

She smiled at him. "Well, I'm challenging your ability to make coffee," she replied.

"And yet, you're drinking said coffee."

Her eyes narrowed suspiciously. "Did you watch a video online or something?"

He shrugged, not bothering to answer, secretly irritated that he hadn't thought of that himself. "Are you packed? My pilot is standing by."

A slow grin curled her lips. "I'll figure out how you did it, Your Highness," she warned.

He moved closer. "I'll tell you if you promise to use my first name."

Rachel felt the spark of challenge, among all of the other sparks that were fizzling in the air between them. "Eh," she shrugged nonchalantly. "I don't want to know *that* badly."

With that, she opened a cabinet and grabbed her travel mug. She poured the coffee from her mug into the travel one, then filled it up to the top. "You didn't tell me *why* we're going to Paris. I thought we were working on identifying architectural firms that are capable of handling your university project?"

"We are, but I always visit Paris before starting a project like this," he told her. "Are you ready?"

"Yes. I suppose. Although, I don't understand your agenda, so I don't know if I packed appropriately."

"Don't worry about that," he said and stepped into her bedroom. "If you need anything, we can get it there." And with that, he grabbed her suitcase off of her bed and carried it to the door. "Let's go."

She followed him down the hallway, carrying her tote bag and computer while he carried her suitcase. Rachel could have handled it herself. But since he wanted to carry it, she saw no reason not to let him. And besides, she liked watching him do it. The task seemed to make him more human somehow. Just like making the coffee, which she was still skeptical about, he was more approachable now. Still overwhelming, but human too.

Chapter 6

"So, what other things do you want to learn?"

Rachel looked up from the laptop she'd been working on to blink at him. "I'm sorry?"

He'd been on the phone with someone for the past hour. She hadn't noticed that his phone call had finished. They were flying to Paris and she absolutely loved the luxury of the plane. It was smaller than the plane that had flown her from Padar to Izara, but still amazingly plush and decadent. The royal family definitely traveled in style!

"You told me that you want to learn to dance and ride horses. What other things are you teaching yourself?"

She rested her hands on the leather armrests, her fingers grateful for the rest from the summary she'd been typing up.

"Well, I've always wanted to speak French and Spanish fluently. But I can't seem to find the time to do that. Every once in a while, I study a verb or two, but I haven't found a way for me to practice often enough for it to make an impact on my progress."

"What else?"

She shrugged. "I want to know how to defend myself. As a single woman," she didn't add that she'd probably be single for a long time. "I know that it's important to know how to fight off an attacker. So, that's another skill I want to practice. I don't have a regular schedule, so I can't find a self-defense class where I can learn the skills." She shrugged. "And that isn't something I can learn online by myself."

He nodded and she wondered what he was thinking.

Fortunately, it didn't take long for him to explain.

"I'll teach you," he announced.

"Teach me?"

"I'll teach you self-defense in the morning before we start working."

Rachel stiffened with horror. "Um...no, that's okay."

He shook his head, waving aside her argument. "I think it's an excellent idea."

Before she could argue further, his phone rang and he took the call. Rachel watched as he stood up, pacing as he spoke, circling the table where they were working.

She was fascinated by the way he moved with such amazing grace for a man so tall and muscular. He looked like a dangerous panther, but she also knew that he was a bit of a tease.

More humanity, she thought with a mental grimace. She needed to stop thinking like that. The man was gorgeous and all that, but he wouldn't be interested in a mouse like her. She was too timid and she wasn't glamorous like the women she'd see him paired with in pictures online.

Getting back to work, she focused on the project and not on the man who looked...decadently delicious.

They landed in Paris and were immediately taken to the hotel. But he didn't give her a chance to open her computer again.

"We need to hurry," he told her.

She looked up at him, startled once again. "We do?"

"Yep. Come along. You won't need your work stuff."

"Where are we going?" she asked, grabbing her tote bag, which also acted as her purse.

"The Eiffel Tower," he announced.

They were back in the limousine and driving through the gorgeous streets of Paris towards the famous monument. "Why are we going to the Eiffel Tower?"

"Because it's one of my favorite places," he replied easily.

"Why?"

"Because I like it. And it fascinates me. I appreciate the way the design connects with the earth and enables the wind. It's one of the ugliest and most beautiful structures in the world, in my opinion."

She tilted her head. "Ugly?"

He shrugged. "It's just a massive steel structure. Did you know that it was built for the World's Fair?"

"Same with the Space Needle in Seattle, Washington," she replied.

"That's another one that I like to visit, but The Eiffel Tower is still my favorite."

"You like this one even more than the huge, elaborate building designs that have emerged over the past few years?"

He nodded enthusiastically. "Think about it. The buildings that are going up now are all done with computers. The architects design something and then a computer does all of the calculations, another computer cuts the materials, and yet another computer monitors the construction. Back in the eighteen hundreds, when The Eiffel Tower was built, there weren't any computers. All of the calculations were done by hand. They didn't even have a calculator." He shook his head, pausing to consider the architectural feat. "It's amazing. I also think the massive cathedrals around the world are just as remarkable. Those were done by uneducated stone cutters without computers too." He winked at her. "That's why we're also visiting Montmartre this afternoon."

Her eyes widened. "We are?"

"Yeah. It's another architectural feat."

The limousine pulled up outside of the tower and a uniformed staff member smiled in greeting as they stepped out onto the sidewalk. "*Bonjour*, Your Highness," the staff member greeted him. "*Je m'appelle Elizabet et...*" they had a rapid fire conversation in French while Rachel listened, irritated with herself for not having a better grasp on the language. Meanwhile, Tarin spoke the language like a native, fluently conversing with the woman, who smiled flirtatiously up at him.

At the end of the conversation, he put a hand to the small of Rachel's back and led her towards the monument. "She said that the officials offered a private tour, but I explained that I'd already visited several times over the years and just wanted to visit the top."

"And?" she prompted when he didn't continue.

He looked down at her, amused at her annoyed expression, which only ruffled her further, and went on. "She said that we'll have a private elevator to the top and can spend as much time as we'd like there, although other visitors will also be present."

"Is that okay?" she asked, glancing at his guards who were walking in a perimeter around them.

"Of course," he assured her. But Rachel wasn't convinced. "But..."

He pulled her closer. "The security team is pretty good at what they do," he assured her as they stepped into elevator. "But I'm flattered that you care. Maybe if you cared just a bit more, you'd actually use my name."

She snorted. "Not gonna happen."

He laughed and she shivered at the sound, hoping that he didn't understand what that shiver meant. It would be beyond humiliating for him to know how she felt about him.

The elevator doors opened and she pulled back, startled to find they were at the top of the tower.

"Coming?" he asked when she pressed her shoulders back against the wall of the elevator while everyone else stepped out.

"Um…" she peeked out at the city skyline through the protective fencing surrounding the top of the tower. "I think I'll just stay here," she told him.

He laughed, taking her hands and slowly leading her onto the landing. "It's perfectly safe," he assured her.

"Yeah? When was the last time someone fell off?"

He shook his head. "The only deaths that have occurred here are suicides, honey. Not accidental deaths. It's very safe."

Tentatively, she stepped out and looked down. Thankfully, the floor wasn't made of steel mesh, it was a solid surface. She took one step, then another, slowly inching out of the private elevator. "I guess I should have warned you about my fear of heights," she said, trying to joke.

If she'd looked up at him, she might have noticed the gentleness in his eyes, but Rachel was too focused on watching her step, then peering out at the horizon, almost as if she needed to make sure that her weight wasn't tipping the tower over.

"I'm sorry, Rachel. I should have asked. But come with me. I promise it will be okay." He wrapped an arm around her waist and pulled her against his side, holding her securely against him. "Better?" he asked.

Yes, but she couldn't admit it because her ability to speak fizzled to a halt. Or perhaps it was her brain that fizzled at his touch. Too terrified to care, she pressed against him, wrapping her arms around his waist in what might be considered a death grip, but she didn't care. He rubbed her back, helping to assure her that she was safe.

When she finally found the courage to look up, Rachel gasped. All of Paris was laid out before her, the sun making the city shimmer and gleam. Because it was a clear day with low humidity, the view seemed to go on forever!

"Oh my!" she whispered, her fear of heights pushed away as awe poured over her. "That's beautiful!"

"Yeah. I agree," he replied. Tightening his arms around her, he nodded towards the distance. "There's the Seine over there, which means that Notre Dame is…" he shifted slightly, "over there." He squeezed her waist. "It doesn't look like much during the daytime, especially after the fire. I'll have to bring you back at night, so that you can see everything lit up."

She shivered just thinking about coming up here at night. "I'm fine right now. Everything is so pretty during the daytime."

Tarin chuckled, thinking that Rachel was far more interesting than he'd thought. Yes, the sexual attraction was still there, but at the moment, with her fear of heights more prominent in his mind, she was soft and sweet, clinging to him as if she trusted him. For a man, that was a heady combination.

"I love being up here," he said smiling as her arms tightened around his waist. "It's such an amazing view, but more than that, the architectural knowledge needed to build this structure is mind-boggling. Plus, I can see all of the other buildings around Paris that were built centuries ago. It's such a shame about the fire at Notre Dame. I would have liked to show you that."

Rachel turned her face up to his and, with the wind whipping around them, her body pressed against his, he wanted to lean down and kiss her. The urge was almost overpowering. The moment stretched, their pulses keeping time together. He looked at her mouth, noticed her lips soften, as if she were anticipating his kiss. He moved slightly so that they were facing each other and saw that her gaze had dropped to his mouth. Was she waiting for the kiss as well? Tarin leaned down and....

Someone bumped him, shattering the fragile moment. Pulling back, he shifted again so that they were looking out at the view. Unfortunately, his mind was still on the lost kiss, still wondering what it would feel like to taste her lips. Would she melt against him?

He sighed, staring out at the views but...they weren't as interesting anymore. Not nearly as interesting as kissing Rachel. Feeling her press her softness against him while knowing that she was his woman would be...unimaginably heady.

"We should go," he said, abruptly turning, but keeping his arm around her waist to protect her from the milling crowd.

The private staff elevator was waiting and whisked them to the ground level. "Merci," he said to Elizabet and shook her hand. "I appreciate the speedy in and out with your assistance."

She smiled, glanced at Rachel with a tinge of envy since Rachel was still in his arms, still pressed against him even though they were safely on the ground.

Unfortunately, the jealous glance must have alerted Rachel of her current position because she jerked away, and smoothed her hands down over her dress.

They made their wait back to the SUV and Tarin took her hand as she stepped into the vehicle. He paused, watching her cute butt as she ducked down, but the view quickly disappeared when she found her seat.

With a silent groan, Tarin followed, sitting next to her and wishing he could take her hand or, even better, pull her onto his lap. Instead, he focused on the next stop. "Now to Montmartre."

"I've never even seen Montmartre," she said, primly folding her hands in her lap.

He looked at her, intrigued by the formal demeanor after such a sweetly affectionate reaction on the tower.

"Are you prepared to climb?"

She blinked and pushed her glasses higher up onto her nose. "Climb?"

"Yep. There are three hundred steps up to the cathedral." He chuckled at her grimace. "Relax. I'll get you a crepe at the base, so you'll be full of energy."

That seemed to perk her up and she looked out the window eagerly. "A crepe? A *real* crepe?" she whispered with excitement.

He smiled at her eagerness. "Have you never had a crepe made from a street vendor?"

She shook her head, those corkscrew curls dancing around her cheeks and his fingers itched to catch one, feel its texture. In the dim light of the palace, her hair looked auburn-brown. But in the sunlight, there were sparks of red, and he was fascinated by the difference. She continued to spark his interest in unexpected ways.

"No. I'm from Georgia. We don't really have street vendors where I come from. There might be some hot dog vendors in Atlanta. And we have some interesting foods at the state fair, of course. But nothing like handmade crepes!"

He chuckled. "There are some who think of the hot dogs in New York as a delicacy."

She squinched up her nose. "I've read about what goes into hot dogs. No thank you!"

"I agree, but they do seem iconic."

"I'm not even sure that there's actual meat in a hot dog. At least, not meat that I'd eat if it were put on my plate. So no, I'll pass."

The SUV driver pulled up to the curb and Tarin stepped out, then turned to hand her out. Rachel hesitated, but he didn't relent, waiting patiently for her hand. When she placed it in his, he tightened his fingers around hers, watching her reaction. Sure enough, just as had happened up in the tower, her expression changed, her lips softened and her eyes brightened with awareness.

Excellent, he thought. He hadn't planned to seduce the lovely woman, but when she looked at him like that, he knew that she burned with the same desire he felt. Tarin vowed not to rush her though. He'd take things slowly and if she felt pressured in any way, he'd back off.

With that plan in place, he tucked her hand onto his arm and led her over to one of the street vendors. "*Duex crepes au chocolat, s'il vous plait,*" he said to the vendor.

Rachel watched the vendor, utterly fascinated, and Tarin watched Rachel as the man scooped the egg mixture onto the flat heating surface, then lifted a wooden tool and smoothed the egg mixture into a large circle. The crepe cooked quickly and the man flipped it over, then added real chocolate pieces to the center.

Tarin watched as Rachel licked her lips, leaning forward like a small child eager for candy. Once again, she'd surprised him with her eagerness, her lack of guile. And especially, her appetite. He couldn't stand it when women picked at a pile of lettuce leaves, looking like skeletons. Rachel was slender, but she obviously didn't starve herself.

When the vendor handed her a crepe, Tarin watched as she took her first bite, holding his own as he waited for her verdict.

"Oh, this is amazing!" she whispered reverently, licking a bit of chocolate from the corner of her mouth.

He watched as she ate, his thoughts once again off into a sexual fantasy. Would it always be like this with her? Wasn't there anything she could do that would keep his mind away from making love to her?

Probably not, he sighed and ate his own crepe, not really tasting it since he was still focused on that mouth of hers.

"Let's go," he groaned, taking their trash and tossing it into a nearby trashcan. With that, he took her hand. "Ready?"

Rachel looked up at the long hillside. There were two ways to get to the top. Up those stairs or via the trolley-like thing that toted people up the hillside. There was a long line for the trolley, so she glanced back up the stairs. "I should have worn different shoes for this, but..." With a smile, she nodded up at him. "Ready!"

With a grin, he started up the stairs. By the time they reached the top, she was gasping for breath. He seemed like he'd just strolled around the block. He wasn't out of breath, not even sweating a little.

"You could at least pretend that you're a bit winded," Rachel grumbled as she glared up at him.

He laughed. "Sorry, honey. You could always join me for a workout in the morning."

Rachel looked up at him, wondering if it was a sexual workout. Or was that just where her mind had gone?

Fortunately, Tarin didn't give her much time to wonder. "Come on inside. It's beautiful!"

They walked along the courtyard and Rachel looked around, stunned by the crowd. People were sitting and picnicking, laughing, talking, debating or just milling casually around. For some, it didn't appear as if they were doing much other than reading or relaxing. "Seems like a lot of tourists," she commented.

"A lot of them are students who come up here to sit in the sunshine or artists who want to sketch the city," he replied.

Inside, the cathedral was quiet and dark, but astonishingly beautiful. In the narthex area, there weren't pews, but instead, moveable chairs were lined up, as if waiting for parishioners to arrive. And yet, the main draw of her gaze was the enormous mural on the domed ceiling.

"It's beautiful!" she whispered, walking alongside him.

"Montmartre is actually the name of the hill and the surrounding area," Tarin told her as he led her through the cathedral. "This church is called the Basilica of the Sacred Heart, or Sacre-Coeur."

"I like it," she smiled up at him. "And you have an amazing French accent. How did you learn the language?"

"Again, one of those princely lessons we all have to learn." He took her hand and led her down one of the pews to sit down. "This place was built over eight hundred years ago." He shook his head in amazement. "*How* did they do it? With all that we've learned over the past eight hundred years, *how* did the architects build something this amazing? Something that has endured for centuries?"

She'd never really thought about it through that lens before. "I can't imagine," Rachel replied honestly, then turned to look up at him. "If you didn't have your royal responsibilities, would you be building things?"

He paused thoughtfully. And then he nodded slowly. "Yes. Most likely."

She smiled, feeling a bit sad for him. Not too sad because…well, because he was a freaking prince who lived a life of luxury, servants catering to his every whim, and the ability to travel wherever he wanted. She still hadn't figured out how he'd made the coffee this morning, but she was fairly certain that he hadn't done it. No way!

"So, being in charge of the infrastructure of the country was the next best thing?"

He shrugged. "In a way."

"Do you ever regret it?"

"No. We all have burdens that we have to face. Did you have an ideal childhood? Are you doing your dream job right now?"

The happiness faded from her eyes and she looked away. "No. You're right."

Tarin paused, but instead of explaining, she closed off, hunching her shoulders. "What just happened, Rachel?" he asked. "What was your dream?"

For a moment, he didn't think she was going to answer him. She stared out at the windows, but he doubted she was really seeing them.

Finally, she answered, "I wanted to be a ballerina," she admitted, sighing and fighting back the ridiculous sensation of feeling...somehow robbed. "I loved dancing. I loved the music and the movement and feeling the rhythm."

"What happened?"

She shrugged and stood up. "I wasn't good enough." She walked out of the cathedral, blinking as the sun shone down on her.

"How do you know that you weren't good enough?"

She shrugged dismissively again. "My family explained it to me. Everyone has dreams. You didn't get yours. I didn't get mine."

He pulled her to a stop. "I'm sorry, Rachel. I suspect that the loss of your dream was more difficult than mine."

She squinted up at him. "Probably not, Your Highness. You get to look around at buildings every day and wonder what it would be like to have built them yourself. And over the next several days, you're interviewing various architectural firms, asking them to do the very thing that you craved to do yourself."

"How is that worse?"

She smiled up at him, trying to pretend that her heart wasn't aching. "I don't see dancers all the time," she explained succinctly. "So, I'm not reminded of the loss of my dream like you are."

He shook his head. "You're not a horrible dancer, Rachel. I don't know what went on in your life before, but you're an extremely good dancer."

She shrugged. "Yes, well, it was a dream. Dancers don't really make enough money to live on anyway, so it wasn't a realistic dream. And it's a very competitive career. I was smart and studied hard in school, got good grades and now," she paused, looking up at the beautiful blue sky with small puffs of white clouds. "I'm happy with my job and my life."

He eyed her carefully and Rachel squirmed under the weight of his gaze, feeling as if he could see what she kept carefully hidden. "Someone convinced you to give up on your dream." He moved to stand in front of her. "Who was it?"

Her eyes shuttered and she looked out across the skyline of Paris. "This is a much better view than from the top of the tower," she said, purposely changing the subject. "I like it here. It isn't so high up that it's scary."

He frowned, but she refused to budge. "Ready to go?" she asked.

He sighed and turned. "Fine. But this conversation isn't over."

She wondered why he even cared. But she was also relieved that he was willing to drop the subject, at least for the moment. "So what's next? I know that you've scheduled meetings with two architectural firms. But...?"

"There's something I want to show you first."

They walked down the three hundred steps, but instead of getting into the waiting SUV, he led her down the street, making a few turns, and then...he stopped.

"What is that?" she gasped, staring up at what looked like a bronze man coming out of a stone wall.

"It's called 'Le Passe Murielle'. It's about a man, named Duteille, who suddenly discovered that he could pass through walls. He was imprisoned at one point, but still snuck out through the walls at night only to be back in the morning, confusing the warden. He had an affair with a woman, sneaking through walls to avoid detection from her husband. But eventually, he lost his ability to pass through the walls and got stuck. So, here he rests, stuck in the stone wall for eternity, cursed to stare out at everyone who walks by. He'll live his life here, unmoving and frozen in time."

Rachel stared up at the bronze statue, her heart thudding in her chest. "How desperately sad," she whispered. "What a magical gift, to be able to pass through walls like that. And yet, to find himself stuck forever. The gift turned into a curse."

"That's awfully poetic, Rachel," he teased, leaning forward.

She blushed and looked away. "I used to be romantic," she said, flicking her hair over her shoulder. "Then I..."

"Then you were told you can't dance," he finished after she paused. Tarin took her hand and led her to the waiting SUV, helping her inside. "Back to business," he announced.

Rachel was grateful to start working. The three tourist stops in Paris had been wonderful, but after her revelations about her dreams –she had no idea why she'd told Prince Tarin about that– she wanted to get back to her normal routines, lose herself in her job. Working projects like this wasn't her dream job, but she gained a great deal of satisfaction in doing her job, in managing the details, and ensuring that projects came together smoothly.

It wasn't dancing, but it paid a whole lot better!

Chapter 7

Rachel couldn't believe her ears!

For the second morning in a row, she'd awoken to someone pounding on her door.

Pushing the blankets back, she peered out at the window. It was still dark outside. Another hard knock and she rolled over to check the time on her cell phone which was propped up next to her on the nightstand.

It was only five o'clock in the morning. Much too early to get up, she decided, and pulled the covers up over her head.

She'd been asleep for perhaps three seconds when she heard the door open. She sat up and looked around, trying to figure out what was happening.

"Rise and shine, beautiful!"

Rachel pushed the hair out of her eyes, trying to figure out if she was awake or not. Since she'd been dreaming about Tarin all night, his presence in her bedroom was confusing, to say the least.

"Tarin?"

His soft, husky laughter sent a thrill through her already dream-charged body.

"At least you call me by my first name when you're half asleep. But it's time to wake up, honey."

"I'm awake!" she yelped. Rachel continued to sit there, looking around as if she wasn't quite sure what was going on. Blinking, she looked at the dimly lit room, trying to make sense of the world. Unfortunately, her brain was too tired and wasn't cooperating. "But...*why* am I awake?"

"Because you're coming with me. Don't worry about showering yet. Put on some exercise clothes and come on out." Then he was gone and she was alone in the dark, cozy room.

She stared at the closed door, running the words over in her mind again. No shower. Exercise clothes. "Why would I do that?" she asked rhetorically.

Out of curiosity, she pushed the covers off and slipped out of bed. Grabbing her silk robe, she padded barefoot down the hallway to the large living room of the hotel suite.

Thinking she'd only dreamed about Tarin coming into her room, she blinked, trying to adjust to the brighter lights out here. Sure enough, Tarin stood in the living room, drinking a cup of coffee and reading a newspaper, pacing back and forth. He looked up when she entered, his gaze moving over her figure and she knew that she'd made a mistake.

"You're going to work out in that?" he teased. "I like it. Might not be too practical though."

She blinked owlishly at his teasing grin, still trying to make sense of this. "What's going on? My alarm doesn't go off for another hour."

He walked over to her, tossing the newspaper onto a table. "I'm teaching you self-defense this morning."

"Self-defense?"

"Yes. But only if you get dressed in something that you can move easily in. As much as I like the robe, I don't think it will stay on once you start trying to flip me over your shoulder."

Rachel had been eyeing the steaming coffee mug in his hand, but with that news, she looked lower, her gaze devouring his chest and arms and all of those muscles. "Um...will I get to do that?"

"Eventually," he teased.

Now what did that mean?

"Do you have any sweatpants or leggings that you can work out in?"

She did, but did she want to wear them around him! "Yes, but...."

"Good. Go put them on. Hurry up, we only have an hour before we need to get ready for our first meeting."

For some reason, Rachel blindly turned around and headed back into her room. She pulled on the leggings and, because she would be around Tarin, she brushed her hair and brushed her teeth, pulling her hair up into a tight ponytail to keep her mop of frizzy curls out of the way. Just for good measure, she swished with mouthwash, not wanting even a hint of morning breath.

She grabbed a sports bra and a tee shirt, pulling both on over her head, then hurried back out to the main room.

"Will this work?" she asked, then regretted asking as his gaze moved up and down her figure, pausing on her breasts, which immediately started tingling, just as they had last night in her dream. But Rachel knew better than to look down to check. She was fairly sure that he was aware of anything going on in her chest area. Looking at herself would only bring more attention to the problem.

"Yes. That will work," he turned towards the door. "Let's go."

"Where are we going?" she asked, jogging to catch up with him.

"To the hotel gym. There's more room down there and we don't have to worry about you throwing me into anything," he teased.

She laughed, rolling her eyes. "Right."

"You never know," he pressed the button on the elevator. "I'm a pretty good teacher."

A half hour later, Rachel had to agree. "Keep your stance loose," he repeated. "Don't tense up in a dangerous situation." He moved closer, circling her. "Okay, come at me."

"No," she groaned, shaking her head for emphasis.

"Rachel, you're never going to learn to take down someone bigger than you if you don't keep practicing."

She'd *been* practicing. For the past thirty plus minutes, she'd been trying to take him down with the arm-twisting method he'd shown her. But he was a foot taller than her and probably more than a hundred pounds heavier, all of it muscle. Now that she was with him and he wasn't in one of his yummy, sexy business suits, she could more clearly see each and every one of those hard-packed muscles. And...wow! Just wow!

"Come on, Rachel, you're not concentrating."

She sighed. She was concentrating all right. Just not on trying to take him down.

Suddenly, he stood up. "How about if we concentrate on something else?"

That was probably a good idea. "Like what?" she asked, thinking coffee would be an excellent thing to concentrate on. Yep, she could really concentrate on a cup of coffee.

"Instead of trying to flip me, how about if we work on close-in attacks?"

That didn't sound like coffee. "What do you mean?"

He moved behind her and she knew this wasn't a good idea. Definitely not good!

"I've been trying to show you how to stop someone coming at you with a direct attack. What would you do if I came up from behind like this?" he asked, wrapping his strong, incredibly wonderful, and oh-so hard arms around her shoulders. "What would you do?"

Besides lean back against him? Oh. Right. Defend herself. Nope, leaning back against her attacker wasn't a good idea. But...yes, it would be lovely if her attacker was Tarin. Especially if he had a cup of coffee!

"Well, I'd probably…" she stopped, realizing she wasn't sure what to do. "Scream really loud?" she offered weakly. Rachel blamed her lack of inspiration on a lack of coffee and not on the fact that this man had done this to her in her dreams last night, but with a completely different ending in mind.

"You're not concentrating," he said, his lips brushing her ear. "You're distracted and that's going to put you in a vulnerable situation. You have to be aware of your surroundings and know what to do."

She wiggled, unaware of the impact her movement had on his body. "Maybe…pretend to faint?"

She felt his smile as his arms tightened. "Then you're just a heap on the ground and in a more vulnerable position."

Frantically, Rachel tried to remember what that one self-defense class had taught her way back in high school. Of course, in high school, she hadn't been addicted to the beauty of coffee, so she'd been paying more attention.

"Isn't there something about the inside of a person's foot?"

"Yes. What is it?" he asked, his arm tightening as he pulled her against his chest.

"Um…shouldn't I stomp on it?"

"Yes. Five minutes ago. Or you could reach up and poke at my eyes," he suggested, his arm moving slightly. His hold felt more…sensuous now. Not at all threatening.

"Or your groin?"

He laughed. "Yeah. The groin on a man is pretty important. A good target, but you can't really reach my groin easily in this position. So, what are you going to do?"

Licking her lips, she frantically fought the fog of desire that was overwhelming her thoughts. "I have no idea, Your Highness," she finally admitted.

"Why don't you use your elbow?"

She thought about that, but shook her head. "I don't want to hurt you."

He laughed, his arm tightening, but again, it didn't feel scary. It felt… really good! She loved being held like this. If she closed her eyes, she could pretend that he was her lover and he'd just come up behind her and…maybe he would kiss her neck. Or nibble on her ear. And slide his hand around to her stomach and…

Jerking upright, she spun around, pulling out of his arms. "I'm sorry!" she gasped.

"For what?"

She blinked at him, then looked around at the others in the gym.

There were only two other people in the gym, both running on tread-mills. "Um...well, I guess I wasn't paying attention."

He moved closer. "You were on the right track. How about if we try again tomorrow and I'll show you more basic moves?"

She nodded. "Right. Tomorrow. Basic." She nodded stupidly, then turned around, almost tripping over her feet. She righted herself, glanced back at him, then hurriedly walked away, terrified that he'd notice the blush staining her cheeks.

Back up in the suite, she sighed with happiness when she spotted the coffee tray that had been delivered while they were working out.

"Good morning, Ms. Morris," a voice called out from behind her.

Rachel was so intent on pouring herself a cup of coffee that she shrieked and spun around, startled. That's when she spotted the other woman, who was just as surprised. After a brief moment, they shared a rueful laugh.

"You okay?" Tarin demanded, bursting into the room.

"I'm fine," Rachel said. "I just..." she waved towards the other woman.

"My apologies, Your Highness. I'm the housekeeper and cook. I stepped out to ask Ms. Morris if she wanted something for breakfast and didn't announce myself properly."

Rachel shook her head. "No, it was my fault. I'd been down with the big guy," she said, pointing her thumb towards Tarin, "and wasn't con-centrating on anything other than getting a cup of coffee."

Tarin frowned at her and she could almost read his mind. "I know!" she sighed. "You were just warning me to always be aware of my sur-roundings." She lifted her cup of coffee. "I *was* completely aware. Of the scent of coffee!" she explained. Feeling foolish, Rachel cradled her cup of coffee and headed for her bedroom.

Tarin watched Rachel leave, appreciating the view of her remarkably fine derriere outlined by the tight leggings. He didn't have to hide his lust since she wasn't paying attention. Her entire focus was on her cof-fee. The woman had zero situational awareness.

Frustration was like a burn along his entire body. Tarin suddenly remembered the presence of the housekeeper. "Thank you, we'll have breakfast in about thirty minutes."

The woman nodded. "Very good, Your Highness," she replied with a dip of her head, then backed out of the room.

Tarin walked over to the silver coffee urn and poured himself a cup of coffee, then took it to his room, thinking that he needed a cold shower. His idea of giving Rachel lessons in self-defense had been a good one, initially. It would help her get to know him better and he would be free to touch her while giving her very valuable information.

Unfortunately, he hadn't counted on desire surging through him every time he touched her or the soft, sexy way she wiggled against him when she was trying to figure out how to get out of whatever hold he'd put her in. Wrapping his arms around her had been a mixture of heaven and hell.

Turning on the shower, he switched the water temperature over to cold in an effort to get his body back under control.

A half hour later, he felt mildly better. That is, until he walked out and spotted Rachel in another one of those flouncy, flowered dresses. This one was a soft green that echoed the color of her eyes. The huge, pink flowers brought out the red highlights in her hair and the V neckline reminded him how much he liked her breasts!

He almost snorted at that last thought. As if he'd ever forgotten how much he liked her breasts! Hell, they'd been pressed against his arm yesterday while on the tower and several times over the course of the afternoon, he'd seen glimpses of her red bra. Why she'd worn a red bra yesterday while wearing a navy dress, he had no clue. But it had been on his mind all day.

Now, he wondered what color bra and panties she wore today. Would they be pink like the flowers on her dress? Or had she chosen a contrasting color, such as she'd done yesterday?

The mystery was going to drive him crazy!

"Good morning," she called to him, bright and sunny now that she'd had a couple cups of coffee. Meanwhile, he was grouchy and irritable since the cold shower had barely clamped down on his raging libido. And the image of her in that moss-green dress had completely obliterated the effects of that damn, cold shower.

Thankfully, the work day started and, because they weren't touring the city, it was easier to concentrate. They met with two architectural firms that day and three construction firms. He also got to sit with her during meals to discuss the contractors, listen to her opinion as well as her impressions, and Tarin was impressed with her insights.

Rachel walked into the beautiful hotel, exhausted and ready to curl up with a good book, then fall asleep. Because of her earlier than normal wake up call, the extra energy exerted during their morning self-defense class, plus working so hard today, she was wiped out! Completely mentally trashed!

"Are you hungry?" he asked as he followed her into the suite.

Rachel turned to look up at him, then quickly away when he tugged at the tie knot, revealing that sexy Adam's apple. "Not really." What in the world? A man's Adam's apple wasn't sexy!

Tarin pressed a few buttons on a screen and music flowed through the room. "Better?" he asked.

Rachel closed her eyes as the soft, lilting music soothed her exhausted soul. "Yes!" she sighed.

"Come. Let's dance," he reached for her hand.

Rachel hesitated. "Dance?"

He hauled her out of the chair she'd slumped into. "Of course. You know the basics of the fox trot. What better way to unwind at the end of a long day?"

With a smoothness that seemed at odds with his height and brawn, he pulled her into his arms, one hand on her waist and the other held her fingers lightly.

"I don't think we should…"

His voice was husky as he murmured, "Don't think, Rachel. Just feel." And he spun her before pulling her close again and Rachel's heart pulsed with happiness and awareness.

Gliding around the suite, Rachel's nervousness melted away as she moved through the steps. His lead was strong enough that she knew what he would do almost before he indicated the next move.

"Just relax," he soothed when she stumbled slightly on a turn. "Let your instincts take over. Stop thinking."

She laughed slightly, trying to pretend that her stumble was caused by her ineptitude and not because she'd felt his chest brush against her breasts.

The music changed and she looked up into his hazel eyes, wondering… a lot of things. Like what it would be like to kiss him. Was his chest as hard as it looked? Yes, from this morning's lessons, she knew with absolute certainty that it was, but she wanted to touch it again. Although, this time with her hands. What would he do if she asked to touch him…No, she couldn't do that. Never!

"What are you thinking about?"

Rachel stumbled over his feet, but his hands tightened, holding her steady.

"Must be something interesting," he teased.

She blinked, her heart racing. "I was just…"

"Just?"

She shook her head. "It wasn't anything important," she whispered back, but her gaze dropped to his lips, her breath catching in her throat.

He paused for a moment, not in the dancing, but the pause was there in his eyes and Rachel was transfixed. Mesmerized.

"I suspect that your thoughts are very important, Rachel," he replied softly.

His words, combined with the heated look in his eyes, warmed a small piece of her soul. Too many times, her thoughts or opinions had been mocked. It hadn't been until she'd moved to Izara that she'd started to feel valuable. Now, in Tarin's arms, small, fluttery wings opened a bit. Those wings fluttered, tentatively feeling the warmth of his pleasure.

"Thank you."

His eyes widened slightly as they moved around the room, seeming to float as their bodies moved in perfect synchronization. "For what?"

She shrugged. "Just...thank you." Rachel didn't want to tell him that she was grateful for his belief in her. Or for valuing her. Those were words that he wouldn't understand, coming from his background. So instead, she stopped thinking and simply allowed herself to lose herself in the music.

Chapter 8

Rachel stepped into the suite in San Francisco, looking around warily. She'd left Tarin talking with the architects, saying she had some personal errands she needed to get done. He'd eyed her curiously, but had nodded, so she'd taken a taxi back to the hotel.

Listening to the blissful silence, she moved slowly towards her bedroom, wanting to just...not move! After almost two weeks in Tarin's presence, with early morning self-defense classes and evening dancing lessons, she was sore in ways she'd never known possible!

Not to mention, the whole trip had been a long series of sexual frustration. Tarin's touch was too much for her these days. She couldn't take more of it before she exploded and begged him to...what? Make love to her?

For a long moment, she considered. Would he? There had been long, powerful moments when he'd looked at her as if he felt the pulse-pounding desire as well. But was she imagining it?

"Probably not," she muttered as she slipped off her heels and hobbled across the lush carpet.

That was another thing! She hated hotel rooms! They'd traveled to Paris, London, New York City, Dallas, and were now in San Francisco. Rachel had traveled with Princess Talia plenty of times. But their trips had been one or two cities at a time, not a marathon tour of five or six! The tedious series of lovely hotel suites that were all beginning to blur together. All of the airports definitely looked too similar for her to remember where they were, and she now understood why airport terminals had the name of the city in huge letters somewhere easy to see. It was for travelers like them, who'd been in too many cities and needed the reminder.

She wanted to go home, she thought wistfully.

"What's wrong?"

Rachel spun around, startled when she heard Tarin's deep voice. "I thought you were going out to dinner with the architects," she said, not even trying to hide her irritation. She had been looking forward to a hot bath to soothe her sore muscles. If he were here, she couldn't have that bath! He'd want do something active, something that would require use of her muscles!

He moved deeper into the room. "I watched the way you walked out of the building and canceled the dinner. Something is wrong!"

He peered down at her, obviously concerned. "Tell me what's wrong. Are you sick?" he asked, pressing his palm to her forehead.

"I'm not sick," she said, pulling back but he only pressed his other hand to the back of her neck, still taking her temperature with his hand. "I don't have a fever, I'm just..."

Rachel pressed her lips together, utterly frustrated. She wanted to be strong and capable and to keep up with him. But right now, all she wanted was an hour to herself, neck deep in the tub.

His eyes narrowed at her hesitation. "Just what? What's going on?"

"I'm sore!" she snapped, losing her grip on her temper. "You're all..." she waved her hand in the air, "physical and moving around all the time, and I'm more of a home body. Normally, I come home from work and I curl up in a chair to read or sew or just relax. There's no relaxing with you!" she finished, throwing her hands up in the air in exasperation.

He blinked at her for a long, stunned moment, then threw back his head, laughing. He pulled her into his arms and Rachel leaned into him, inhaling the clean, masculine scent of him. Goodness, he smelled good and felt good and sounded sexy as hell! For a precious moment, she closed her eyes, leaning into his hard chest, reveling in the moment.

"You need a massage," he told her softly.

Jerking away, she shook her head. "Nope! No massage," she told him firmly.

He lifted a dark eyebrow as he looked down at her. "You don't like massages?"

She shivered at the intensity in those eyes of his, but wrapped her arms over her stomach defensively. "Um...I've never had one before," Rachel admitted. At his astonished look, she continued, "The idea of being naked while a stranger touches me is..." Rachel stopped abruptly, realizing where that statement was going. She grimaced when she looked up at his raised eyebrows. "Okay, that sounded weird."

He laughed softly, moving forward. "I've pushed you much harder this week than you're used to, haven't I?"

She leaned back against the wall behind her. "Yes. But that's okay."

He moved closer, standing directly in front of her. "Now you're sore and achy...and afraid of a massage."

Her body stiffened at his charge, but since she really was sore, the effort only caused her muscles to protest. It was worse when he reached out to slide a finger along her jawline. "Will you let me make it better?"

Rachel closed her eyes, leaning into that touch. Just for a moment, she promised. Just for the sheer pleasure that it gave to her tired, aching body. Then she realized what she was doing and her eyes flew open, her lungs filled with air, and she tried to pull back. But he realized what she'd done! Looking into his eyes, they were...heated?

"I'm fine," she told him, trying to pretend as if that moment hadn't happened.

"You're more than fine," he replied, his voice rough and low. His legs now touched hers and the skirt of her dress danced around his slacks. Their clothing was a barely adequate barrier to the tension vibrating around them.

But then he stepped back abruptly, turning away from her. "A massage will fix your aching muscles. Pressing the lactic acid out will release it and help ease the pain and it will also help them heal." He walked to the bar. "I'll get you a glass of wine while the massage table is brought up to your room." With that, he poured a glass of scotch for himself and white wine for her.

When Tarin looked over at her, still standing there against the wall, she jerked upright. "Thank you, but I don't need a massage." With a curt nod, Rachel hurried down the hallway to her room.

"I'm just going to take a hot bath and that will fix all of my problems."

Turning on the water, she sat on the side of the tub as she stripped off her clothes, dumping them on the floor because she was just too sore to put them away. When the tub was half full, she used some of the bubble bath on a whim. Normally, she didn't allow herself the luxury of bubbles. But tonight, she poured them in with a heavy hand, feeling extra decadent.

She'd just slipped into the hot water, closing her eyes and leaning her head back against the tub when a knock sounded. "I'm fine, thank you!" she yelled, assuming it was the housekeeper.

The door opened and Tarin stepped into the bathroom. A moment ago, the bathroom had been decadently large, but with his huge frame standing by the tub, the room shrunk!

"What are you doing in here?" she gasped, trying to gather the bubbles closer, hiding her nudity.

He set a glass of white wine on the edge of the tub. "Just bringing this in for you," he said, then glanced at the floor and froze.

Rachel knew exactly what he was looking at. In slow motion, she watched as he bent down and picked it up. When he straightened, there was a pretty pink bra with small sparkly gems dangling from the spot between the barely-there cups. "Is this what you were wearing today?" he asked softly.

Her eyes widened, but she couldn't form the words to respond. When he looked down at her, his eyes moved over the bubbles, obviously trying to see through them, and compare what he saw there to the small bra. "Nice," was all he said, then turned around, walking out of the bathroom. "The massage table is ready when you are. Just come on out in your robe."

Then he closed the door. Biting her lip, she struggled to come to terms with one thing; he'd kept her bra! The man had stuffed her pink bra, one of her favorites, into his pocket!

Rachel took a fortifying sip of her wine, leaning back against the tub again. But after his visit, the warm bath was too warm. It wasn't relaxing. She turned her head and wondered about the massage. Should she do it? What harm could there be? She'd never had a massage before, so maybe she could indulge. Just this once?

Stepping out of the bathroom, she eyed the long, cushioned table with the soft sheet draped over it. There was a note that instructed her to cover herself with the sheet and lay face down. Sitting right next to the table was a cart with oils that looked to be in some sort of warming system and the whole thing looked…surprisingly inviting.

"Fine!" she grumbled. Dropping her robe, she moved to the table and took the sheet, shaking it out and draping it over her body as she lay down. The soft music and dim lights relaxed her more than the bath had.

She heard the door open and felt hands on her foot, trailing along her leg.

"This is my first time," she told the person.

"You'll be fine," Tarin's deep voice assured her.

Instantly, Rachel stiffened and tried to sit up. But his firm hand on her shoulders gently pressed her back down. "Don't worry, Rachel. This will feel good." He chose one of the bottles of heated oil and spread some in his hands.

"Tarin, this isn't…!"

He leaned down, very close to her ear. "Relax, Rachel. I'm *very* good at this." He put his hands on her shoulders and slowly pressed into the stiff muscles there. Immediately, she felt the pressure ease and moaned. "Wow!" she sighed, relaxing into his hands.

"I told you I know what I'm doing," he replied with a laugh.

"Good grief, that feels incredible!" she sighed blissfully, as his strong fingers pressed into her sore muscles.

He continued to knead the knots in her shoulders and, when those were soft and pliant, he moved to her arms, starting with the right before moving to the left. He even pressed the tips of his fingers along her hands, stretching each finger carefully. As he returned to her back, she sighed with relief as he pressed into the small of her back. He soothed the muscles and every bit of tension in Rachel's body released, easing with the pressure of his hands.

There was sexual awareness too, but with the way his hands were moving over her body, in an assured, non-sexual way, she could push the awareness to the back of her mind.

He moved higher, pressing his thumbs into the muscles along her spine and her shoulders, then lower and lower on her back but, when he started to get too low, she shifted, tensing slightly.

His soft chuckle washed over her. "Too low?" he asked, tugging the sheet higher, covering her whole back. That's when he moved to her feet, pressing against the arch and her heel, her toes, in places she hadn't even realized she was tense until he pressed a thumb or the heel of his hand into that spot. When he finished with her feet, he moved up one calf, then the other. He didn't venture higher than her knee and she appreciated that. Any higher than her knee was dangerous territory.

"Still okay?"

"Yes," she sighed sleepily.

"Good," he replied. "I'm going to pick you up and put you into bed now, okay?"

"Oh!" she gasped, starting to sit up, surprised at how sleepy she was. "I can..."

"Be quiet," he ordered softly. He carefully lifted her up, wrapping the sheet around her as he went, and tucked her into the bed. "Go to sleep, Rachel. I'll see you in the morning," and with that, he turned off the lights, bent low to kiss her sweetly and disappeared, closing the door behind him.

Rachel smiled as she rolled over, hugging a pillow to her chest. She really should get up and pull on her pajamas. But just now, she was disinclined to move. So she sighed and snuggled deeper into the warmth of the bedding and promised herself she'd just close her eyes for a moment, then get up and put on some clothes.

Chapter 9

Rachel woke with a start, looking around at the sunshine streaming in through the huge windows in her bedroom. For a long moment, she couldn't remember where she was. The sheets were white, the curtains white, the furniture white…everything in the room was white.

Then everything came back to her and she remembered. San Francisco. The massage! Tarin tucking her into bed last night with a sweet kiss goodnight. Just thinking about that kiss made her heart glow with tenderness.

"Not love!" she gasped, then sat up, not sure where that thought had come from. Looking around, she tried to orient herself, but the sheets wrapped around her legs made extricating herself from the bed difficult. Pushing everything off, she padded into the bathroom and stared at her image in the mirror. It wasn't too bad, she decided. The mascara looked a little panda-ish, but her hair wasn't going off in crazy directions.

She picked up her clothes from the previous night while she waited for the water to warm up in the shower. That's when she noticed that her favorite pink bra wasn't amidst the other clothes. And then she remembered the pink bra dangling prettily from Tarin's finger last night. And that he'd stuffed it into his pocket!

Good grief, how was she to get her bra back? And why had he taken it?!

The questions continued to mount and she needed coffee in order to process. Stepping into the shower, she sighed as the warm water washed over her skin. "Saturday," she whispered as she squeezed some shower gel into her hands and started scrubbing. "It's Saturday and…" she closed her eyes, trying to remember Tarin's schedule. "No meetings." With a sigh of relief, she smiled. "It's Saturday and we don't have anything scheduled today." She shampooed and conditioned her hair, considering possible activities. She didn't need to do laundry because everything she wore was magically cleaned and returned to her closet the following morning. She didn't need to pack because there were other magical people who would do that when they left. But Tarin still had meetings in San Francisco on Monday, so they'd most likely stay here over the weekend. Would he want to review the notes she'd taken? Probably, she thought with increasing dread.

Normally, Rachel loved her job. But after the marathon meetings and traveling over the past ten days, plus being with Tarin all day long, including for every meal, plus his self-defense lessons every morning and his dancing lessons in the evening...both of which she loved and, Rachel even acknowledged to herself that she was getting better at both...but she was wiped out! She needed a break.

Oh for the opportunity to just sit on a sofa with a good book and read all day long!

"Not gonna happen," she muttered as she stepped out of the shower and dried herself off. Glancing at the time, she wondered if Tarin was even here now. It was well past nine o'clock in the morning. That was pretty late, considering that he normally rose before five o'clock to head to the hotel gym to work out every morning. She suspected that he'd already gone through his brutal workout and was showered and off to... whatever it was that royal princes do on the weekends in foreign cities.

Pulling on a pair of leggings and, because the temperature was only getting up into the mid-fifties today, a sweatshirt, she grabbed a pair of thick socks and quickly brushed her hair, then dabbed on a touch of makeup. Just in case he was still here, she told herself.

"Just to look professional," she whispered to the mirror. "The makeup has nothing to do with my emotional stupidity."

Stepping out of her bedroom, she walked down the hallway, not exactly sure how she was going to face Tarin this morning. If he was even here, she thought with increasing hope.

Unfortunately, her hope was dashed as soon as she stepped into the main living area of the suite. Tarin was there, reading a newspaper and drinking coffee.

He was hidden behind the newspaper and, for a moment, she considered slipping away and hiding in her bedroom to wait him out. Last night's massage and...well, everything else seemed to be a good topic to avoid. But she also knew Tarin and he wasn't the kind who avoided problems. He confronted them head-on.

"Not gonna work, Rachel," he called out, not even lowering the newspaper.

Darn it! How had he known she was standing here? And how had he read her mind so easily?

Scary man.

"I wasn't..."

His paper flipped down and he folded it up, tossing it onto the low coffee table in front of him. "You were trying to avoid seeing me after last night, weren't you?"

Yes! "No. Absolutely not."

"Good. Then come get your coffee and let's talk."

Rachel was torn. The coffee was on the other side of the living room, over towards the dining room table. But safety was behind her. She'd have to walk all the way across the room with him watching her. Cowardly? You betcha! And unashamed.

"I think I'd rather..."

"We need to talk," he told her, cutting off whatever she was going to say. "Get some coffee, Rachel," he repeated, then stood up, resting his hands on his hips. "We need to clear up a few things."

Taking a deep breath, she stepped forward, her stomach sinking with dread. Was he going to fire her? Did he realize the depth of her feelings for him? Surely he couldn't know that she lo...*liked* him in that way. But he was a bit more intuitive than she was. Perhaps he'd noticed something she hadn't even realized was happening.

Nothing to do about it other than tough it out. So instead of standing there like the coward she was, Rachel lifted her chin and walked slowly, steadily across the room. Pouring herself a cup of coffee, she picked it up, then took the porcelain cup out of the saucer since it was shaking so badly, it was rattling.

"Nervous?" he asked when she sat down across from him.

She debated lying to him, but took a deep breath and nodded. "Terrified," she confirmed.

"About what?"

"About this conversation. Are you going to fire me?" she asked. That was probably for the best, she thought. Being fired would at least get her away from him. She didn't need to have feelings for a man so completely out of her league.

"No! I'm not going to fire you. There's no reason to fire you and you're the best project manager I've ever worked with."

"Oh," she whispered, startled by his praise. She'd vaguely hoped that she'd been doing a good job over the past few weeks. But he hadn't said anything. "Um...thank you."

"You know that you're outstanding. You're excellent with details and regularly see things that I missed. So, don't *ever* doubt your worth,

Rachel. You're good and you should know that by now."

Wow! That was incredibly high praise!

Cradling her coffee, she stared across the coffee table at him. "So… what's this conversation about?"

"It can't have missed your attention that I want you." He stated that so clearly, as if the statement wasn't like a bomb that had just been dropped into the room. "Sexually."

Woah! "Um…!" Rachel lowered her eyes, feeling her cheeks blossom with burning color. "That's…!" Amazing! Exciting! Shocking! Oh and terrifying too! Yep, totally terrifying!

"Give me your honesty, Rachel. I need to hear how you feel about me."

She looked up, directly into his hazel eyes. "Your…"

"Rachel, I had my hands all over your body last night and I put you to bed." He paused, letting that image settle between the two of them. His voice deepened as he said, "I'm hoping to do the same tonight, but I'm also hoping that I'll be in that bed with you this time. So, it's way too late for you to use my title now. It's past time for you to use my first name."

Rachel looked at him, contemplating her answer. "How about this. I'll use your first name when we're in private, but when we're out in public, I use your title."

He leaned back against the sofa, stretching his arms out across the cushions as he contemplated her for a long moment. "So, you want to hide our relationship?"

She shifted slightly, shaking her head. "At the moment, we only have a professional relationship."

Those too-knowing eyes narrowed on her. "You and I both know that's going to change. Today."

"I don't know that at all," she countered, her green eyes challenging now. "Last night, you…touched me. But that's nothing new. We've been working closely together for the past…"

"Don't," he interrupted. "You and I both know that last night was different. And if you are going to sit over there looking lovely and tempting, then I'm going to have to head over there and prove to you that things have changed. That we're both aware of the sexual intensity that literally throbs every time we're in the same room."

She nibbled her lip. Should she be honest with him? But if she did, would there be anything left? And…would he laugh at her? He'd said that he wanted her, but for how long? She wasn't the kind of woman who held a man's interest, especially not someone as intense and powerful as Prince Tarin!

And yet, as she watched him, debating how to respond, Rachel knew that she had to be honest with him. "Yes. I feel it. But I don't think we should pursue a personal relationship."

Instead of becoming offended or angry, as another man might, Tarin simply tilted his head to the side. "Why not?"

Rachel set her cup down on the coffee table. "Because I'm not made that way. I don't do casual relationships. You might be able to do that. But with me, relationships are very personal. They have to be, otherwise, I'm not interested."

His eyes brightened as if she'd just confirmed his suspicions.

"So, you're saying that you already have feelings for me." It was a statement, not a question.

Rachel swallowed, looking down at her hands folded in front of her. "I...don't know." That was about as honest as she could be at the moment. "You scare me...Tarin." There! She'd said it! She'd used his name!

Wow, it felt...liberating and terrifying, both at the same time!

"Feels good, doesn't it?" he teased.

"No!" she countered. "You are a scary man, Tarin. I don't think I could ever fit into your world. And that doesn't make me feel good about contemplating a relationship with you."

He moved over to sit beside her. "Okay, so you're scared. So am I," he told her, taking her hand.

She snorted, shaking her head. "That's a lie. You've never been scared of anything in your life. Admit it."

He shrugged. "I've always been bigger than most of my peers. But my older brother used to scare me."

She rolled her eyes. "I doubt it. What could your brother possibly do that would scare you?"

"He draws."

Rachel heard him, but the terrifying Sheik Amit el Raminar...drawing? "No way!"

"Yep. When he's stressed about something, he just picks up his notebook and draws anything and everything. He used to draw monsters and scary stuff, and would leave the pictures on our beds." Tarin shook his head. "Scared the sh...I was scared," he finished with a chuckle. "My brother has an incredible imagination. Plus, he'd convinced us that he could only draw things that he could see. And he'd tell us that he'd seen the monsters in our closets or under our beds."

She laughed, delighted with this glimpse into Tarin's childhood. "That sounds horrible. What did you do?"

He shrugged. "I stayed up some nights, waiting for the monsters to show themselves. Then my parents would get angry with me for falling asleep at the breakfast table. I'd tell them what Amit had done and then he'd get into trouble. He'd then make a scarier drawing and the whole process would start over."

She giggled, slapping a hand over her mouth. "That sounds awful. You were mean siblings."

"You have a sister. What was it like growing up with her?" he asked, taking her hand and turning it over so that he could trace pictures on her palm.

Her laughter died and she looked away. "Oh, my sister and I never really got along. She was...special."

"And you're not?"

She smiled, but the expression revealed a deep sadness. Not wanting to talk about this, Rachel curled her fingers into a fist so that he couldn't tease her anymore. But he only pressed her fingers back, touching her and sliding his fingers up and down her hand and arm.

"Tell me," he urged, continuing to tease her hand. Rachel felt his touch echo through her body. "What's so 'special' about your sister?"

She sighed. "My sister is truly beautiful and very talented. Anything she tackles, she excels at. It was difficult growing up in her shadow sometimes." Most times, she silently added.

"What did she excel at?"

She shrugged, standing up and stepping away. Wrapping her arms protectively around her waist, she looked out the window. "I don't know. Everything." She took a deep breath and turned back to smile at him. "Would you mind if we changed the subject?"

"Back to the two of us having sex? Absolutely!"

She laughed. "Well, maybe we could ease into that conversation."

"I was thinking we could ease into the relationship," he replied, standing up and walking over to her. "I loved touching you last night. Your body is beautiful, Rachel."

She snorted. "You should see how gorgeous my sister is. She has softer hair and she really knows how to put makeup on to enhance..."

He reached out to touch her, just a palm to her cheek, but it was enough to shock her into silence. "I don't care about your sister, Rachel. And just for the record, I think you're beautiful." He stepped closer and she stared at the middle of his chest, unable to meet his gaze. "I love the way your eyes are huge and expressive," he said, his thumb caressing her cheekbone. "And your nose is pretty darn adorable."

She smiled, wanting to shake her head to deny his comment, but she didn't want to risk losing his touch. "You don't understand, my sister is..."

He stopped her argument with a kiss. Rachel was so startled she couldn't move. She even forgot to breathe. He didn't kiss her again, but he didn't move back either. Their lips hovered just a hair's breadth apart. Rachel waited, wondering if he'd do it again. She wanted him to kiss her more than anything she'd ever wanted in her life. But she trembled, wondering if she *should* want this. Was she worthy of his kiss? Would he like the way she kissed or would he hate it? Was she completely inept at kissing?

"Rachel," he whispered and she felt his breath wash over her face, felt the need in him as well and lifted her eyes from his mouth to his hazel eyes. That was all it took. Instead of pulling back, she leaned in and kissed him. No more waiting! No more self-condemnation! This was her moment! This was Tarin and she'd lo...wanted him for so long!

That must have been what he was waiting for because, at the first touch of her lips against his, he wrapped those massive arms around her waist and lifted her higher, holding her against his hard chest! He deepened the kiss as Rachel wrapped her arms around his neck and kissed him back. She wasn't great at kissing, not having much experience with it. But Tarin didn't seem to mind.

She felt one of his hands move to the back of her head, tangling in her hair and tilting her head back, deepening the kiss even more. She squeaked, unaware of how her legs wrapped around his waist as she trembled, unconsciously grinding against him and moaning with every frisson of sensation. She felt his erection against her core and was startled for a long moment, pulling away from him and looking around.

"We're..." She realized that they were sitting on the couch and she was straddling his hips, wantonly riding him.

"Yes. We're kissing," he groaned, his hands sliding up and down her waist, down to her thighs then back up

Rachel told herself to get off of him, that she was smothering him. But the way his hands skimmed over her body felt too good. Staring at him, unaware of the look of need burning in her eyes, she shifted deliberately against that hardness. Just a small movement but...she gasped, her hands gripping his shoulders.

"Rachel!" Tarin groaned, his fingers tightening on her hips. But he wasn't sure if he was holding her in order to stop her from moving like that, or...waiting for her to do it again.

She took the decision out of his hands when she leaned in to kiss him again and her hips shifted with the movement. He couldn't hold back, not after that moment of boldness. He'd thought she'd be a shy, tentative lover. He'd anticipated encouraging her to enjoy her sexuality.

So this bold, wild woman was...stunning! He wanted to ravage her, explore every inch of her skin and...howl at how hot she was! But words wouldn't come, so instead, he rolled them over until she was on her back and she stared up at him with those huge, green eyes of hers. The look was both humbling and igniting!

She shifted her hips again and he almost lost control. Pulling back, he moved his mouth against her neck, her shoulders but that damn sweatshirt was in the way. So, he pulled her upright so that she was straddling his hips, then pulled the shirt over her head and out of the way.

Then froze! "Every day, I've wondered what you were wearing underneath those prim flowered dresses of yours," he told her, entranced by the pretty blue bra. There were yellow daisies embroidered along the edge and he lifted a finger to trace those flowers.

"It's padded," he noticed.

"Yes," she replied, her voice barely above a whisper.

She was watching him, watching his hands against her breasts. Turning his hand, he cupped her breast.

"Why do you need a padded bra?"

She rolled her hips against his erection again and he saw her eyes blur, her tongue dart out to wet her lips.

"Because...I don't want...anything...showing through my dresses," she finally explained.

"I want to see your nipples," he announced, then released the catch on her bra, tossing the scrap of blue and daisies away.

She hissed in surprise when her bra was gone, but he ignored that, focusing on her pretty breasts and, especially, those beautiful nipples, so taut and pointing right at him, as if they were begging for his attention.

He reached out, cupping them again, but this time without the hindrance of her bra. As he cupped both breasts, he looked into her eyes, then slowly, as if savoring the moment, ran his thumb over those taut nipples. He smiled evilly when she hissed in reaction, so he did it again. And again. Her head fell back as he continued to tease her breasts, taking one nipple into his mouth and sucking lightly, then nipping it with his teeth before soothing it with his tongue. Every caress caused yet another, and her hips couldn't keep still. It was possibly the most erotic moment he'd ever seen.

Unfortunately, kissing her wasn't going to be enough.

Scooping her up, he carried her into his bedroom.

"What...?" she asked, looking around. But by that time, he was already kicking the door closed behind them.

"I don't want the hotel staff to see you, Rachel," he warned, then leaned down, laying her in the middle of the bed.

"Oh, right," she breathed, looking around. "But..."

Tarin couldn't wait. Not with her pretty breasts and tight nipples staring at him. So he kissed her, his mouth moving over hers until he felt her melt against him. Only then did he lift his mouth and resume his exploration of her breasts. With every touch, every kiss, nip, and teasing touch, Rachel gasped and hissed and ground herself against him, driving him wild with lust.

Trying very hard to go slowly, he moved his mouth lower, kissing along her stomach while pulling her leggings off. But not her panties. Oh no! He needed to see her in whatever sexy little nothing she'd pulled on this morning.

When he stood up after tossing her leggings off to the side, he stared down at the piece of blue satin with little daises. "Do you always match your bra and panties?" he asked, letting his finger trail along the edge of her daises.

She gasped and did a sexy little wiggle thing. "Yes," she hissed. His finger slid under the elastic. "No!"

"No?" he teased, letting his finger linger there. "You don't always match your panties to your bra?"

Her pink tongue darted out, wetting her lips and he might have smiled, but he was so turned on, he wasn't even sure he was breathing.

"I don't...!" She hissed when his finger slid into her body, her hips lifting as if she were offering herself to him.

"Tell me," he growled, watching her face as he teased, thrusting his finger in and out.

Her eyes were closed. He let his thumb flick against that swollen nub and she gasped, her hand whipping out to grab his wrist. But he didn't relent, wanting to know what turned her on, what she liked and what she didn't. So far, everything he'd done seemed to be good.

"Don't stop!" she moaned, pressing his hand against her.

With a muttered curse, he pulled away and literally ripped that piece of blue satin off. When he heard a muttered cry from Rachel, he moved up and kissed her. Hard! "I promise to replace all of your lingerie, love. But..." he pulled back, shaking his head to try and disperse the almost painful lust overwhelming him. "Just...trust me, honey."

With that, he moved back down her body, kissing and exploring, finding a few more spots that made her cry out. But his ultimate goal was that beautiful, throbbing nub between her legs.

"Tarin, I...!" she cried out when he pressed her legs wider.

"I have to, Rachel," he explained, his voice barely above a growl. "I have to give you this now, because once I get inside you, I'm not sure how long I'll last." And with that, he kissed his way from her knee to her inner thigh, then to that place he'd wanted to taste ever since he'd gotten her through the door to his bedroom.

Unfortunately, as soon as his mouth touched her there, she exploded and he barely got a taste before she was throbbing with her first release, her fingers tangling in his hair.

When she finally relaxed, he pulled his mouth away, kissing her stomach again before he stood up and stripped off his clothes. Grabbing a condom, he looked down at her, feeling like a king after what he'd just done to her.

With the condom rolled down over his erection, he moved back between her legs, bracing his hands on either side of her head as he kissed her, bringing her back to him.

"Do you have any idea how beautiful that was?" he asked, but didn't give her time to answer. Instead, he pressed into her folds, closing his eyes as her body accepted his. Deeper and deeper, he pressed into her until he was fully inside of her.

He reached for her hair, his fingers tangling in those amazing curls as he began thrusting. With every movement, he heard her mewling, gasping and groaning, driving him even wilder. Faster and faster, he thrust into her until...with every fiber of his being, he held on until he felt her body tighten around his shaft. But after that, he pounded into her tight sheath as his body emptied into hers, his mind draining of everything but the intense, incredible pleasure!

The pinpricks of her nails was his first taste of reality. And it wasn't that he felt her nails so much as he registered the absence of her fingernails as her hands slowly unclenched from his shoulders.

Her soft sigh reminded him that he was too heavy for her and he groaned, rolling over but holding her, shifting so that her replete body was draped over his. Then his hands dove right back into those amazing curls of hers.

"So soft," he muttered.

Rachel was still a bit dazed and he smiled up at the ceiling, thinking, "I did that!"

But her hair wasn't the only soft thing about Rachel. Her back, her waist...her whole body was soft as silk.

"Tarin," she sighed, wiggling again.

Tarin laughed softly. Lifting up, he kissed her. "I'll be right back," he promised, then carefully extricated himself, heading for the bathroom. Quickly, he cleaned up, then came back...only to come to a complete stop. Rachel looked...beautiful! Her auburn curls were going every which way, and her surprisingly long legs were curved, making her butt look extraordinarily enticing. And since she still hadn't revived after those two orgasms, there was a soft, satisfied smile to her lovely features and his body hardened, just watching her.

She yawned, blinking like a small, sexy kitten. "I should..."

"You should stay right there," he growled, coming back to the bed and pulling her back on top of him.

"I'm pretty sure this isn't dignified," she grumbled, but her wiggles only turned him on all over again.

"I'm pretty sure that you should do that again," he laughed, sliding his hands along her bottom, then higher, trailing a finger along her spine.

She gasped, arching her back, which only reminded him that he hadn't fully explored her back.

But he was more interested in her breasts and rolled over so that she was underneath him. "Yes?" he asked, not really paying attention. He was fully focused on her breasts. On those taut, pink nipples that whispered to him.

"I need..." she stopped speaking when his mouth covered her breast.

"Coffee," he teased. "Right. You need coffee." But he didn't stop. And a moment later, she didn't care as he started the whole process over again.

About two hours later, he finally got her that coffee.

Chapter 10

Rachel beamed as she walked into the meeting Monday morning. Life was good. In fact, the whole world seemed to glow lately. Glancing over her shoulder, she spotted Tarin talking to one of the directors of the architectural firm. He must have felt her gaze because he paused in his conversation and looked in her direction.

Was it just her, or did his gaze warm when he looked at her? Quickly, Rachel glanced away and focused on...she looked down, trying to remember what she was doing. Right, she was handing out briefings. She'd done this several times over the past few weeks. The briefing outlined the university project's requirements, although the briefing was just a rough outline of the criteria. Neither the buildings nor the layout of the campus had been designed yet, nor had anyone even offered a layout. This was a multi-billion dollar project so the firms would submit bids to run the effort in Izara starting next month. At least, that was the plan. Rachel wondered if perhaps...?

No, that wasn't her place. She was here to offer operational and financial analysis support. She'd keep her opinions to herself.

Smiling, she finished handing out the briefings, then took a chair set back against the wall near the window. This was the last company that they'd talk with and Rachel admired Tarin for what he was doing. Not only was he including firms from all over the world to bid on the project, but he was going to them, discussing his vision in their space. Not for convenience. Goodness, it definitely wasn't convenient for him to travel from city to city talking with each firm individually. Nope, he flew thousands of miles and went over this briefing so many times because he wanted to meet with the potential firms on their turf, to get a feel for their style. He didn't want anything to be anonymous. He wanted a personal touch.

She blushed as she thought about the way he'd personally touched her just this morning. Tarin had been ravenous and she couldn't count the number of times she'd climaxed in his arms. With her arms pinned over her head. Or with his mouth. Or...!

Focus! She snapped to attention and looked up, only to find Tarin watching her, his pen pressed against his mouth and...he knew! He knew that she'd been thinking about this morning and...darn it, a blush heated her cheeks again. Drat the man!

She hated that she was so transparent, but when it came to Tarin, she was pretty much lost. Saturday and Sunday, they'd mostly stayed in bed, talking and teasing each other, learning what each other liked, how each of them preferred to be touched and teased. Goodness, he was a tender and demanding lover! She'd only been with two other men in her life and neither of them had really turned her on. Not even close to the way she felt with Tarin

Looking around, she avoided Tarin's eyes this time and stared intently at the speaker, jotting down pertinent points as they were brought up. These meetings were about the strength of the firm, the way they managed their projects and their building "philosophy". Sometimes she chuckled at the silly ways they phrased their pitches to Tarin. Some of the firms came up with the most ridiculous catch phrases, but in a weird way, those firms also stood out in her mind. She wondered if that was also true with Tarin. Was it better to have silly phrases that stood out? That showed that they were creative and weren't afraid to experiment. Or should firms stick with their strengths? That indicated that they relied on solid, tried-and-true building methods.

Her sister did both. Denise was one of those women who had so many strengths, she just...was like a shiny diamond, all flash and hard as a rock. Meanwhile, Rachel considered herself more of an opal. She wasn't flashy. Nor was she tough and hard. Opals seemed to sparkle from the inside. Their shine was more subtle, but...looking over at Tarin, she realized that she was pretty. She sparkled. Not like her sister, Denise. But in her way, which was just as valuable. It was different, but still beautiful.

Sitting up in her chair, she pulled her shoulders back. She was an opal, someone with a fire inside of her. Just as good as a diamond, but different.

Tarin's head swiveled in her direction when she shifted, his eyes narrowing for a moment.

Feeling good now that she'd compared herself to an opal, she smiled back at him, feeling confident and powerful. Beautiful. She *was* beautiful in her own way. Rachel almost laughed out loud when he shifted uncomfortably in his own chair and she knew what he was thinking!

A long time later, after lunch had been delivered and consumed, more conversations about the details of the university project and more pronouncements that this particular firm could accomplish the job with elegance and finesse, the meeting ended. This one had seemed longer than the others, but that might be because she and Tarin were eager to get away.

Unfortunately, even after leaving the meeting, they still weren't alone. There was still the car ride back to the hotel, although sitting in the back seat, Tarin reached over and took her hand. It felt sweet and innocent, although she knew that it wasn't. Looking up at him, she felt the spark of need in him mirroring her own.

They were silent during the drive. Neither spoke in the elevator since they were surrounded by his body guards. Outside the suite, she waited for the guard to unlock the door, to check with the guards inside the suite. And then she waited while the guards vacated, finally leaving them alone.

But the moment the door to the suite closed behind them, it was as if the magnetic forces of their bodies took over. She threw herself at him and he carried her to the bedroom, kissing her as she clung to him. Tumbling onto the bed, they frantically stripped their clothes off, touching each other as skin was revealed.

When he entered her this time, she froze, feeling the incredible fullness and it was so blissfully prefect, neither of them wanted to move. Looking down at her, Tarin's hands curved around her head, tangling in her hair. A moment later, he shifted inside of her, filling her up again, only to retreat. Rachel arched her back when he moved away, then wrapped her legs tighter around his waist. Again and again, he drove into her body, pushing their pleasure higher and higher.

"Tarin!" she whispered, urging him to stop teasing. Unaware she did so, she dug her fingernails into his shoulders and he understood. After being apart for most of the day, there was a driving, demanding need for that blissful finale. He thrust into her, knowing how to move against her to maximize her pleasure.

Rachel arched against his body, taking his thrusts into her as her body climbed to that peak, and…then she screamed as her body throbbed with a release so intense, she was blinded for several moments. Rachel felt him stiffen and she tried to increase his pleasure, but her body was just too far gone, too far into her own climax to help him.

When he collapsed against her, Rachel wrapped her arms around his neck, keeping her legs around his waist. She beamed at the beauty of what he could give her every time they came together like this. It was incredible and wonderful. She loved him. After denying her feelings, even to herself, for so long, Rachel reveled in the knowledge that she loved Tarin el Raminar. She hadn't wanted to fall in love with him, and when this was all over, she knew that she'd be shattered. But for this moment, she loved him with all of her heart and being.

With that knowledge, she kissed his shoulder. His ear. His neck. Her fingers skimmed up his back to his shoulders, diving into the softness of his hair.

"Are you okay?" he asked, lifting up onto his elbows.

Rachel laughed, stretching languidly. "I'm better than okay now," she told him, lifting her leg so she could rub her inner thigh along his hip.

"I saw you watching me earlier today," he growled, rolling over and heading for the bathroom. "I knew *exactly* what you were thinking," and he disappeared. She heard the water running and stretched again, pulling the rumpled bedspread higher to cover her nakedness. He might walk around without inhibitions, but Rachel wasn't so blasé.

"And I could see the answering desire in your eyes," she replied, smiling as she grabbed one of the pillows.

He reappeared and climbed back into bed. "Yeah? So, that means you *were* thinking something. Care to share?" he asked, tugging the blanket away so that he could admire her nakedness unhindered. He slid his hands over her stomach in a sensuous, lazy pattern. That was one thing about Tarin that she really appreciated. He loved to touch. A lot of the time, it wasn't even sexual. He just loved touching her. He preferred to have her snuggled against him while they slept. He loved touching her while they ate, maybe tucking her hair behind her ear, or as was the case Sunday night, they'd ordered pizza and ate it curled up together on the bed with one of his arms around her and his back as her pillow.

She really liked this affectionate side of him. It told her that he liked her not just sexually; he also really liked just being with her. It made her feel all warm and gushy inside, which was a completely new feeling.

"Are you ready to go home?" he asked as he pulled her into his arms.

"No," she sighed, snuggling closer and resting her hand on his ridged stomach, her head on his shoulder.

He laughed and she felt it all the way down to her toes. "Me neither," he kissed the top of her head. "Unfortunately, that was the last firm I wanted to talk with, so our preliminary work is done."

She contemplated that, wondering what would happen when they returned to Izara.

"I don't want this to end when we go back home," he told her, reading her mind.

She sat up, gazing into those amazing eyes of his. "You don't?"

A strange expression slipped across his face. "You think we'll have had enough of each other after this?" he asked.

She bit her lip. "No. I don't think that will happen. At least, not on my side of this thing." She didn't add that she doubted she'd ever get over him, never get enough time with him. But he didn't want to hear that. Not from her.

And because she felt so strongly, she needed to show him. Instead of waiting for him to make the first move this time, she shifted, pressing against his chest until he was flat on the bed and threw her leg over his hips. "I don't want this to end," she admitted, kissing his chest, letting her hands slide along his muscles, feeling them ripple under her fingertips. "Not yet, anyway."

Tarin closed his eyes as her soft, tentative lips kissed his chest, hissing when she licked his nipples. Already, he was hard and ready for her. But this was pretty damn nice too. He loved the way she touched him, as if he were something special. Her fingers smoothed over his skin, sliding and exploring, her mouth following, her tongue darting out to taste him. He loved it. He loved every moment of her attention. Hell, he loved her!

Tarin didn't say that. Not yet. She'd run away if he admitted it. In her mind, it was probably too soon for declarations of love. But in his mind, he'd been in love with her forever. At least since that first day she'd walked into his office, asking sweetly for something Talia needed. He'd watched her flowered skirt swish around her legs, so demure and yet, so incredibly sexy!

He hadn't known about her love of sexy underwear back then, and never would have guessed. Knowing now, seeing the way other men looked at her, curious, as if they knew that she was more than just another pretty face, but not sure what it was about her that drew their attention, he wanted to laugh and shout with joy because he knew Rachel's secrets.

She hid herself underneath those flowered dresses and...he even liked that! He loved knowing her secrets and her desires, loved knowing that she gasped when he did certain things.

He'd been floating for several moments, enjoying the way her fingers and mouth moved over his stomach. But he hadn't been paying attention to her other hand...until her fingers wrapped around his shaft!

He almost bolted upright, but those huge, green eyes looked at him, startled and suddenly unsure. "Yes!" he groaned, trying to give her encouragement. But already, he felt like he was going to explode.

"What do you like?" she asked nervously, but with an eager look in her eyes.

"Like this," he rasped, taking her hand and showing her how to move it over his erection. He wanted her mouth on him too, but…! "Damn it Rachel!" he groaned, falling backwards as he felt her hot, wet mouth close over him. Her hand moved and her mouth surrounded him, her tongue caressing and…he couldn't hold back!

"Honey, I can't…!" he tried to pull away, but her hand tightened on his shaft and she sucked harder and…he lost control. He exploded and he fell backwards, his hands gripping her hair carefully for fear of pressing her down too hard during the throes of a climax that was hard and fast and…mind-blowing!

When he had his breath back, he opened his eyes to find her straddling him, watching him with that sexy smile that he loved so much.

"Oh, you are so going to pay for that," he warned a moment before he flipped their positions.

"But…I thought you enjoyed it," she protested, laughing when he grabbed her wrists and held them up over her head, guiding her hands to grip the headboard. His hands immediately cupped her breasts, his mouth covering that sensitive tip and sucking. Hard!

He heard her gasp and didn't relent, moving from one taut peak to the other, making her cry out and arch her body, which only pressed her breasts deeper into his mouth.

Moving lower, he kissed and teased, all the while, pressing her legs wider.

Tarin smiled when she tried to wiggle away from him. She knew what he was about to do. He'd done it to her before. Many times over the past several days. In fact, he loved teasing her core, watching her body come alive to his touch but not letting her reach that release until…until he'd brought her to the edge over and over again.

"Please," she sobbed, trying to get away. But as soon as he took his finger away, she grabbed his wrist.

"You're going to stay still, Rachel," he warned, trying to hide his smile.

"Yes!" she sobbed, pressing her hands against his shoulders until he felt the small pricks of her fingernails. "Yes. I'll be still."

He knew that she wouldn't be, but it turned him on when she tried… and failed.

Moving closer, his mouth covered that nub, flicking it with his tongue and she screamed, fighting to remain still. He pulled away and she smacked her fists against the covers of the bed.

"I won't do it again!" she vowed.

He laughed. "Yes, you will. I loved it. And so did you."

She lifted her head, glaring at him, and he lifted his eyebrows in question. "Then why are you doing this to me?"

He slid a finger along the wet, glistening folds. "Because I like it."

She gritted her teeth and tried to pull back, sliding away from his mouth.

He knew all her tricks though and grabbed her hips, pulling her back into position. "You know that's not going to work, love."

"Please! I can't take much more of this," she begged, combing her fingers through his hair. He smirked, lowering his head again.

"I think you can," and with that warning, he moved closer. But this time, she was too close to the edge and she exploded against his mouth. He loved this, loved feeling her writhe in such an uninhibited way. With his mouth and fingers, he extended her pleasure until she sighed and he pulled back.

Grabbing a condom, he rolled it down over his shaft, then settled himself over her again. "Tell me that you want me," he ordered, pressing against her opening, but not entering her.

She shuddered, wrapping her legs around him. Damn, he loved this woman!

"I want you," she whispered, lifting her hips to meet his thrust. "I want you so much!" she gasped as he pressed into her, filling her up until she arched into him, taking him even deeper into her body.

Then he started thrusting, slowly at first, bringing her back to need. All too soon, she was exploding around him, her inner muscles clamping down on his shaft. Her climax took him right along with her and he filled her up, groaning with his own release.

Chapter 11

Over the next two weeks, Rachel fell further in love with Tarin. Every day, they worked together, and not just on the university project. He brought her in on several other major initiatives that he was working on. She felt as if she were part of the team, especially when he asked her for her opinion. Even his other advisors came to her for assistance, asking for feedback and for her organizational capabilities. She analyzed the financials for the various projects, offered her feedback, provided options, and felt more alive than at any other time in her life.

At night, Tarin took her into his arms and made love to her. She never knew if their lovemaking was going to be wild and frantic, or slow and languorous. Every moment in his company was filled with pleasure of one kind or another.

And after he'd make love to her, he'd turn on music, pull her into his arms and teach her about dancing. She learned the foxtrot and the two step, swing dancing and, one night, he showed her the tango.

"It's a love story," he explained, guiding her into position.

"A dance is a love story?" She looked at him with that teasing glint in her eyes.

"Don't mock," he told her sternly. "This is a battle between the sexes, a love story of the ages." He took her hands and placed one on his shoulder, the other in his own. "It's all about a battle for control." He stepped forward and she instinctively moved backwards. "A battle of love and hatred."

She laughed, but by now, she could anticipate what he would do merely by the way his hands felt on her skin. "A love story about hatred?"

"Absolutely," he replied. "The tango is about the dichotomy between emotions. Hatred and love. Happiness and sadness. Life and death. It's a back and forth, with each emotion, each person, battling for control."

She stumbled a few times, but he merely steadied her against him, causing them to pause as their skin on skin contact aroused them.

"I push you one way, then you push me back, forcing me to listen to you." She moved forward, "pushing" him backwards. "And then I confuse you with a twirl," and he spun her under his arm. She twirled again and again. "But I'm always there to unravel the mysteries," and he caught her in his arms. "But you don't want my power," he explained and pushed her outward, their hands clasping as she extended her arms, "but our love is too strong and we can't fight the battles of the world without each other." He spun her back into his arms. "And then we're back to the dance, again," he explained, moving her forward, then himself backwards.

By the time he dipped her at the end of the dance, arching her over his arm, she was breathless and more turned on than she could ever remember.

"Kiss me, Tarin," she whispered urgently.

They didn't make it to the bed that time and she gasped as he entered her. There was no more foreplay. Just the age old primal dance until they found their release in each other's arms. As he lifted her up and carried her to bed, she leaned her head against his shoulder.

"Who won?" she asked sleepily, snuggling up against him as her eyes drifted closed.

Tarin watched her fade off to sleep, his heart hammering against his chest. "I did," he murmured, turning off the light and holding her until the early hours of the morning, enjoying her soft breath on his skin as he considered the various ways he might convince her to stay with him. Forever.

Chapter 12

Rachel hummed as she walked into her office. She'd been with Tarin for more than a month now and she felt happy. Amazingly happy. She kept trying to find some other word for how she felt, but every time she tried to define her life right now, that word kept popping up. Happy.

The phone ringing brought her out of her happy haze and she lifted the receiver. "This is Rachel Morris," she replied.

"Ms. Morris," a deep voice replied, "This is Sargent Kingsley at the security office. You have visitors that aren't on our list."

His voice was admonishing and Rachel wondered who would dare to arrive at the palace without an official invitation. "I'm so sorry, Mr. Kingsley, but I didn't invite anyone. Whoever...?"

"They identified themselves as your family members. Denise Morris?" He prompted. "And your mother, Pamela Morris and father, Mark Morris."

Rachel went cold. "My *family*?" she whispered blankly. "That's impossible! They live in Georgia. They aren't..."

"Their identification has an Atlanta, Georgia address. Please come to the security office to identify these people."' And with that, the man hung up the phone, obviously irritated that someone who worked in the palace hadn't followed the strict security protocols.

"Rachel, I don't think that..." Tarin paused a foot away from her desk and frowned, trailing off when he saw her expression. "What's wrong?" he demanded, dropping the file and coming around to pull her into his arms. "What's happened? Are you hurt?"

She wound her arms around his waist. "I'm not hurt," she told him. At least not physically, she added silently.

"You're shaking! Tell me what's wrong!"

He waved to his bodyguards, three of whom stepped into the office,

80

scanning the room for threats.

"No!" she gasped, embarrassed. "I'm fine," she assured him.

He stepped back to peer down at her, his hands gripping her upper arms gently, but firmly. "You're not fine. You look like you've seen a ghost and you're shaking like a leaf."

She laid a hand on his chest. "I'm sorry. I just...I got a call from the palace security and...," she closed her eyes. "My family is here. I wasn't expecting them. I'm so sorry."

He looked down at her, not really understanding. "Your family? Here?"

"Yes," she replied, her legs going numb. This wasn't good, she thought. If Tarin saw Denise...he'd be enthralled. Denise had always been the beauty in her family. Denise was lovely and vivacious and wonderful. Denise was the charmer. Rachel always felt like a shadow whenever Denise was around.

"Go collect your family," he ordered a guard. "Escort them to my office."

"No!" she gasped, pulling away, unaware that she was starting to hyperventilate. "I should go. I'm sorry, I'll just...!" Rachel wasn't sure what to do, panic was clouding her thoughts. "I'll find out why they are here and I'll get them settled." She tucked her hair behind her ear, trying to hide her fears.

"Why not bring them here?" he offered. "They can dine with us at the palace tonight."

She shook her head. "No, I don't want to impose," she protested, feeling as if she'd suddenly reverted to formal manners, but she couldn't help it. Her old habits were coming back to her and she couldn't fight the instinctive need to hide.

"It's not a bother, Rachel," he told her softly.

She looked up at him, saw the concern in his eyes and...something snapped inside of her. "I have to go," she told him, blinking back tears of frustration and fear. "Please?"

He sighed, rubbing a hand over the back of his neck. "Fine. But...call me, okay? Let me know how it goes."

She nodded stiffly, then turned away. Grabbing her purse, she hurried towards the door. "I'll let you know as soon as I find out why they arrived unexpectedly."

Tarin watched her leave, frustration boiling in his gut. He felt powerless, which he hated. What the hell was going on? She'd been so happy this morning. But her family shows up and she's suddenly tense and shy? What the hell?

It was a mystery and he hated mysteries. They needed to be solved. So, why the hell was he standing here?

Because he had yet another damn meeting, he realized as his aide stepped into Rachel's office, pointedly checking his watch. Still, Tarin hesitated, looking out the door as if he could somehow see her again. But she was already out of sight.

Damn it, they were so close! Between the two of them, they'd chosen the architectural firm they were going to hire to design the university center. There was a big event planned in a week to announce the project to the rest of the country. He didn't want to do it without Rachel. She'd been instrumental in the planning process, offering suggestions and urging him to promote different building practices that, in the end, would make the university center easier to maintain and more energy efficient. And it was all because of Rachel! She had to be there for the announcement!

She had to be there for *him*. He needed her in his life and couldn't imagine not having her in his arms every night.

So, what was it about her family that created this intense sensation of dread?

Rachel hurried down the various hallways leading to the security office, not seeing the elaborate murals that had been created by some ancient artist centuries ago. Crossing her arms protectively over her stomach, she smiled through the administrative building security process, things she hadn't done in over a month, because she'd been traveling with Tarin. Then, she'd basically moved in with him here at the palace. She still maintained the apartment down the street, but she hadn't been there since she'd left on the two week trip across the world doing the architectural firm interviews.

She should have known that this happiness couldn't last. She wasn't the kind of person who got a happy life! She was the kind of woman who lived in the shadows and...well, Denise was the kind of woman who got to go out and be happy.

Her footsteps slowed as she neared the guard office. Why were they here? They hadn't spoken to her in years and she hadn't bothered to go home. Why? Because she hated how they treated her.

After a childhood of being told she wasn't good enough, she'd finally pulled together the courage to get away, to find a place where she felt good and others considered her work to be worthy. She'd done it! She'd struggled at first, but she'd done it!

So, why were they here now? She didn't want to go back to being that quiet, timid person. The shy, weak person who jumped at shadows.

But her family had this strange power over her. Just one word and....

Rachel stopped in the middle of the hallway. "No!" she said out loud, startling a passing staff member. "Sorry," she whispered to the other person, who hurried away. "I *won't* let them do this to me. Not again!"

She reminded herself that she had choices. She was in control.

With that in mind, she lifted her chin and squared her shoulders. "I can do this," she told herself. With a self-deprecating shake of her head, she continued down the hallway. "How many people have to give themselves a pep talk prior to facing their family?" she muttered.

Placing her hand on the door of the guard office, she paused, took a deep, steadying breath, then opened the door and stepped inside.

Rachel took it all in with a quick glance. Her family. Her mother stood by the window, texting, but looking up to snap orders or criticism at her dejected, silent father who sat nearby. He never bothered to respond. The man simply accepted his wife's nagging and...ignored her. And there was her sister, in all of her astounding glory. With a smile and a slight tilt of her head, Denise had charmed three of the palace guards, who were leaning over the counter, thoroughly entranced.

It was a typical scene, one she'd witnessed so many times throughout her childhood.

Moving deeper into the guard room, she made her presence known. "Hello everyone," she called out, trying to appear cheerful even though she felt sick to her stomach.

Six people turned to look at her and Rachel refused to cower. Not today, she told herself firmly.

"Goodness, Rachel, dear. What in the world are you wearing?" Pamela Morris demanded, stuffing her cell phone into her leather purse. "I would have thought you'd learned to dress more professionally. Those hideous flowered dresses should all be in the trash!"

Rachel steeled herself against her mother's criticism. "My attire isn't the issue today, Mother," she snapped and felt a surge of power when her mother blinked. Rachel's hands fisted at her sides and she felt a sense of pride when she ignored the impulse to clutch the material of her skirt. Lifting her chin, she forced her lips back to a smile. "How are you?"

Her mother shrugged, obviously recovered from Rachel's sharp reply. "Hot, darling! Take us to your apartment so that we can unpack. This godforsaken country is so miserably hot!"

Rachel stared at her mother, shocked that she would be so...blatantly offensive. Turning to the guards, Rachel smiled weakly. "I apologize, she's just..." she trailed off, realizing that she didn't need to apologize for her mother's bad behavior. "She's just a horrible person," she finished, then shrugged as if to say, "Family? What can you do?"

Turning back to her family, she straightened her shoulders. "Right. So, what are you all doing here?"

Pamela snorted. "Can't a mother visit her daughter?"

Rachel considered her words as well as the implications for a long moment. Then shook her head. "Not you."

Her sister laughed, then shifted into her "alpha dog" pose, as Rachel used to think of it. "Don't be a drag, Rachel," Denise purred, moving forward to embrace Rachel, who stood stiffly in her sister's arms. "We're here to see where you work and find out more about your life here. We haven't seen you in what...? Three years? That's an awfully long time to avoid us, don't you think?"

Rachel didn't answer. Instead, she looked at her father. They had always been so similar, but Rachel couldn't imagine living his life, being the object of pity and constant nagging. It was one of the reasons she'd escaped, not wanting to turn into him.

Her gaze returned to her mother, eyebrows raised. "And you're here to visit me...why?"

"Because we miss you, of course," her father spoke up.

Rachel felt a crack in her armor. Could that be true? Had they even noticed she was gone? Probably not. Her mother ran an event planning company in Atlanta. Her father was the accountant and Denise had joined the family business right after she'd graduated from college.

Realizing that she wasn't going to get the truth out of them in front of an audience, she shifted again. "Right. Well, where are you staying?" she asked, then braced herself.

"We're staying with you, of course!" her sister announced with a ridiculing chuckle, as if that were the most obvious answer. "There's plenty of space here, isn't there?" she mocked, her eyes lifting as if she could see through the walls and ceiling of the palace security office.

Rachel saw the guards stiffen but stepped forward. "I don't live here at the palace," she told her family honestly, even though she had been staying here, with Tarin, for the past few weeks. It had been nice, but then again, all good things must come to an end. "I live down the street in a small, two bedroom apartment."

Her mother and sister shared a horrified glance. "Seriously? You don't rate a suite here at the palace?"

Another chunk came out of her armor, but she fought against the pain. "The palace is the home of the royal family."

"Well, can't you find us a place? Surely, they have guest rooms here." Her mother grinned gleefully. "I've always wanted to stay in a palace."

Rachel's fingers tightened, her nails digging into her palms. "You'll need to get a hotel if you're going to stay here in Izara," she told them firmly. "But I suppose you can stay at my place for tonight. But, you'll need to get a hotel tomorrow. There isn't much space in my temporary apartment."

She took out her keys and waved to the guards. "Thank you so much for the call," she said. They nodded professionally as Rachel walked straight through, out of the guard office and back into the late afternoon heat.

Rachel heard a few sputters of surprise before her family members gathered their belongings and followed her. "Well, aren't you going to call someone to carry our luggage?" her mother demanded.

Rachel turned and looked at her family. Her mother had three large suitcases, her sister four. Her father, on the other hand, carried only a small bag and looked ready for whatever adventure was coming his way.

"As I said, I don't live here. I don't have a staff of personnel to carry your luggage." She turned and headed down the long sidewalk that went along the fence line. This area of the palace wasn't landscaped, but it was still neat and tidy. Thankfully, it was functional and practical, planned to accommodate visiting dignitaries and palace guests.

There was a rumbling of bags behind her as she strode down the sidewalk, along with a great deal of grumbling.

"Rachel Morris, you get right back here and help us with our bags!" her mother shrieked. "How dare you just walk away like that! I taught you better, young lady!"

Another crack, and this time, a chunk of her armor fell to the ground. Turning, she looked at her family, willing herself to ignore them just as they'd ignored her for so much of her childhood. But old habits came back to her and, at the familiar shrill tone, she turned back and grabbed the heaviest bag. Thankfully, it was a rolling bag, so it was relatively easy to pull behind her.

"Where is this apartment of yours?" Denise demanded, hurrying to keep up. She was stumbling a bit with her bags, but somehow managed to teeter gracefully on her high heeled sandals.

"It's just...."

Suddenly, a large, black SUV pulled up beside them and a driver got out. Rachel knew at once that Tarin must have dispatched a car and driver for her and she almost broke down in tears. He was such a wonderful man, she thought.

"Ma'am," the driver greeted Rachel. "I'm here to assist your family however I can."

Pamela's furious features smoothed into an elegant smile. But only when she turned towards the driver. When she turned to Rachel, the smile vanished. "There now, was that so hard?" her mother chided, glaring at Rachel. "I swear, Rachel!"

Rachel politely stepped back on the curb as the driver hurried around to the back. The driver loaded the suitcases into the back of the truck, but despite his careful attention, Pamela still snapped at the man, ridiculing his efforts.

"Mother! Stop it! The man is doing a good job!"

Pamela turned around and Rachel gulped. Stalking towards her, Pamela pointed a finger in Rachel's face. "Don't you *ever* speak to me like that again! I will not be humiliated in front of servants and you will do well to treat me with the respect I deserve, young lady!"

With that, she huffed and stepped into the front seat of the SUV, and slammed the door shut.

Her father shuffled closer, shaking his head. "You know how she can be," he murmured. "Remember? We talked about just letting her do her thing?"

Rachel turned to look at her father, stunned by how he'd changed over the past three years. His hair was almost completely grey and there were significant wrinkles around his eyes. His shoulders were more slumped than she remembered and he looked defeated.

"I moved to Izara in order to get away from all of this negativity, Dad."

He sighed, his shoulders drooping even further. "Yeah, I know honey. But your mother needs help with her business. That's why we're here."

Rachel felt rage rising into her throat, choking her. Go back? To that life? Never!

"I won't go back," she told him firmly. "I'm happy and needed here."

He nodded, squinting against the harsh sunlight. "Well, just listen to her, okay?"

With that, he stepped into the back of the SUV and tugged the door closed. Rachel stared at the vehicle, wishing that she were somewhere else. Anywhere else! With a sigh, she walked around to the other side of the vehicle and slipped in beside Denise.

"About time!" her sister huffed, peering at her reflection in a small mirror. "This heat is ruining my makeup."

The driver pulled up outside of the apartment building, leapt out and, before her mother could start complaining, piled the luggage on the sidewalk.

"Thank you," Rachel said to the driver who politely nodded to her, eyed her mother and sister warily, then jumped back into the SUV and sped away, tires squealing.

"Goodness!" her mother snapped, fanning away smoke from the tires.

"Rachel, you need to report that man. That's just dangerous driving."

Rachel sighed as she pulled the keys out of her purse. She hadn't been here in several weeks, so she wasn't sure she remembered what the place looked like. It was probably covered in dust by now. Had she even made her bed? She didn't remember much after Tarin had shown up with the news that they were traveling to Paris.

That seemed like a lifetime ago, she thought wistfully as she led them inside. The elevator ride to her floor was too short and, with dread, Rachel unlocked the apartment door, then stepped back to let everyone inside.

"Goodness, this is tiny!" Her mother shook her head disparagingly. "Rachel, I thought you were doing well. But obviously, if this apartment is any indication, you can't be making much money."

Rachel didn't mention that the apartment wasn't hers or that her real apartment was actually smaller than this one. She wasn't home much due to her long hours, so she'd never felt the need to have a large apartment. Rachel preferred to put most of her money into savings and investment accounts instead.

"We'll take the bedrooms," Pamela announced to Rachel. "You can sleep on the couch."

Rachel opened her mouth to argue, but her mother had already vanished into the master bedroom and shut the door while Denise had disappeared into the second bedroom.

Rachel stood there in the living area, stunned and furious. "How long are you staying?" she asked of her father, who had already taken up his normal position on the couch with the remote in one hand. That's how he survived, she realized. Just sitting in front of the television and ignoring everything as his life slipped by.

He glanced over at her, resignation in his eyes. "That all depends on you, honey."

Rachel huffed a bit, then turned around. "I have to get back to work," she announced. "Here are the keys, so you can get in and out of the apartment." She dropped the keys onto the kitchen counter. "If you need food," she started to say she'd stop by the grocery store after work, but then her gaze landed on the two closed doors. "If you need food, there's a grocery store around the corner."

And with that, she left, feeling strong and proud. She could do this! As Rachel walked back up to the palace, ignoring the afternoon heat beating down on her, she felt power surge through her. She was good at her job, Rachel reminded herself. No way was she going to let her mother and sister make her feel small and useless again. No way!

Chapter 13

After five days of living with her family, Rachel was at her breaking point. She felt small and insignificant. She was exhausted from sleeping on the uncomfortable couch and she was losing the battle against her mother's guilt trips about coming back to Georgia to help with the business.

Tarin walked into her office the following Friday and she ached to feel his arms around her. But she'd kept away from him because her family was so toxic. Illogical as she knew it was, she feared contaminating him.

"What's going on, Rachel?" he asked gently.

Rachel sniffed and looked out the window, giving in to the inevitable. "I have to go back to Atlanta and help my family," she said, her heart breaking with every word.

Tarin stared at her, his heart aching for her. He wanted to pull her into his arms and hold her, but her body language over the past week had screamed 'Hands off'!

"Why?" he asked, wanting to yell at her, but knowing that he had be gentle. He'd received word from several sources about the way her family treated her and he couldn't do the same thing. "You have a job here. One that you're amazing at and you love."

She sniffed back a sob and his heart lurched at the thought of her tears. "Because they...need me."

He sat down in the chair beside her desk, leaning his elbows on his knees. "But I need you. Here."

She shook her head and stared blankly down at the pages in front of her. Brushing her curls off her forehead, she sniffed, struggling to pull herself back together.

For a long moment, he watched as she closed her eyes. But when those green eyes opened again, she was all business.

"The party tonight is all taken care of. The orchestra is setting up now. I've been over the menu one last time with the chef and the food is delicious." She blinked, still fighting the tears. "Everything is set up and ready. Also, the dignitaries have arrived."

"And your family? Are they coming as well?"

"No!" she yelped, shaking her head. "No, you don't want them there. I'll just...I'm leaving with them on Monday, so you won't have to worry about them anymore."

Tarin stood up, pacing across her small office as he struggled to tamp down on his helpless fury at her words. Fear clutched at him, both at what her family had done to her as well as what he would lose if she left. Standing up, he paced the length of her office. "Of course, I'll worry about you. Why are you doing this?" he demanded, pausing to frown at her with his hands fisted on his hips.

"I have to," she replied, bowing her head.

That just didn't make sense! Walking over to her desk, he let his fists rest on her desk. "No you don't!"

"Their business," she explained, desperate for him to understand. "It's failing. I used to work at their event planning business, but...well, they're struggling now."

"It's *their* business. Not yours! You've never once mentioned their business and I know that you don't really care."

He was right! He could see it in her eyes! "My mother...she said she needs me, Tarin."

He paused, eyeing her carefully. "I've told you I need you too."

She blinked again, furious that she couldn't hold back her tears. They spilled over, pouring down her cheeks. "Look, I'm barely coping here now. Please, just let me go. This...thing between us was bound to end at some point. Besides, you need someone who is strong and vital. I'm..." she sighed, her shoulders folding inward. "I'm not good enough for you."

Not good enough?! What was this crap? Her smiles warmed his heart, brought life and sunshine into his days! "Shouldn't I be the one to make that decision for myself?"

Rachel ached all over, and not just because she'd been sleeping on the couch. She missed him so much. "I'll just go check on the arrangements for tonight," she said, walking out of her office and leaving Tarin, and her heart, behind.

"Don't go, Rachel. You know they aren't good for you. Every time they call or you read one of their messages, you're hurt and wounded."

"They are my family, Tarin. I can't turn my back on my family when they need me!"

He slapped the desk, glaring at her with a ferocity that seemed to… excite her? No! That would be wrong! She couldn't be with Tarin. He wasn't her man and…!

"Please, Rachel! They are toxic! Give *us* a chance!"

"It won't work. I'm not…" she bit her lip, wanting to tell him that she wasn't worthy, but as she looked up into his eyes, she wanted to believe she was. She wanted to believe that there could be a future between them. Then her mother's taunting words from this morning came back to her. *"You're just a plaything to him, Rachel. Stop making a fool of yourself and come back home where you belong. You're staring longingly at him like a puppy…well, you're embarrassing yourself and us. It's pathetic because he couldn't possibly return your feelings."* Rachel hated the power her mother and sister had over her. She'd fought it tooth and nail over the past five days, but their attacks were so vicious!

So, why the hell was she even considering going back to help them?

"You are!" he stated with vehemence. "You're worthy and wonderful! Don't leave Izara, Rachel. Stay and…"

"And what?" she asked, pleading with him to say the words that she so desperately needed to hear.

He pulled her closer. "Stay and be with me."

That was nice to hear, but they weren't the words that she needed. She needed him to tell her that he loved her! Rachel was so completely, madly, deeply in love with Tarin, but he just cared for her? It wasn't enough.

In that moment, she knew that she wouldn't return with her mother and sister. They were truly horrible people and, if she went back, Rachel knew that they would destroy her.

But nor could she stay here. She loved Tarin too much to stay. Remaining here at the palace…that would destroy her as well.

She allowed herself a moment to memorize the feeling of his heat against her one last time. But only a moment. This was forbidden territory now, she thought. If she was ever going to get over her love for him, she needed to stop allowing herself these moments. If he'd just tell her that he felt the same way, then maybe…but he hadn't. He'd only asked her not to leave Izara.

"I have to meet with the event staff," she said and carefully extricated herself from his embrace. "Thank you for this time with you," she whispered, looking up at him.

Tarin watched her leave and he wanted to roar with frustration. Where was the feisty woman who had ordered him around two months ago? Where was the hot, sexy siren that had tempted him with her expressions, her hands, and her body? The woman who had laughed when he couldn't figure out how to make coffee and had refused, despite several direct orders, to call him by his first name?!

This woman, this Rachel, was a shell of her former self. No one in the palace ever got the best of her, but a few days with her family and...hell!

He knew that she loved him and he loved her so intensely, he couldn't think straight most of the time. He had to get her away from those horrible people! Even if she chose not to stay with him, those vile excuses for humans would destroy her!

Running a hand over his face, he sighed with frustration. Leaving his office, he hunted for Harper. When he found her, in Amit's office, sitting on his lap, Tarin rolled his eyes.

"You guys have been married for too long to be still doing stuff like that," he grumbled.

Amit glared at his brother. "What do you want? Also, go away."

Harper tried to stand up, but Amit kept his arms around her, holding her on his lap. "What's wrong?" she demanded.

"I need your help," he admitted, his voice almost cracking at the idea of asking anyone for help. Especially when it came to his love life. And yes, that's exactly what it was. Love. He loved Rachel and, even if she didn't stay with him, if she returned to Talia in Padar, he didn't want Rachel to go back with her family. They were horrible and dangerous.

"It's Rachel," he said, perching on the edge of the desk. "Her family is toxic! Everything they do and say is meant to belittle her. It's overt and it's constant. They've only been here a week and already Rachel is being browbeaten back to her shy, timid self instead of the vibrant, confident woman she's been over the past few years. I've heard little comments from them here and there, criticizing the way she dresses or telling her to stand up straight and at least pretend to show some pride." He shook his head with a disgusted snort. "It's horrible, Harper. Tell me what I can do to get her away from them!"

Harper had stood halfway through his explanation, her eyes shifting from smiling to concerned. By the time Tarin finished, she was frowning. "When are they leaving here?"

Tarin stood as well, needing to move. He began pacing the office. "That's the thing. They were only supposed to be here for three days. But they've stayed for a week. Plus, she just told me she's going back with them to help them with their business. Apparently, it has been falling off since she's been here in Izara. They've convinced her to come back and fix things for them." He shook his head. "She can't do it, Harper. Her mother and sister are vile. They do and say everything they can to undermine Rachel's confidence and self-esteem. She's strong though," he added, turning to smile at Harper so that she saw his belief in Rachel. "She's so strong, but it's nearly impossible to block out a family member, even if they are being abusive."

Harper agreed. "It's exactly how abusive men wear down strong women. They start with small comments, little criticisms. Then those comments grow. When the woman tries to pull away, he switches into sweet mode again. It's insipid and painful. So yes, I'm sure Rachel is very strong; she's had to be. But her family has probably convinced her that she's not, that she needs them in order to manage."

"She doesn't need them!" he snapped. "She needs me! And I need her, damn it!"

Harper smiled gently. "Have you told her that?"

"Yes! But she says that she needs to go help her family!" He shook his head, his hands fisted on his hips. "I can't let her do that. I can't let her give up this battle. I love her too much."

"If they were good...?"

He understood where she was going with that prompt and hated it. But he was honest. Closing his eyes, he braced himself for the truth. "Yes. I love her enough that, if they were better for her, I would let her go." He opened his eyes and looked directly at Harper. "I love her. I just want...I *need* her to be happy, Harper."

"That's good." She stepped closer to him. "Think, Tarin. Is there something that can get through to her? Something the two of you have done that made her feel powerful and beautiful? You need that crutch to break their power."

He stared at her and a thought occurred to him. Something that... would it work? It had to work! But even if it didn't, he would never stop fighting for her. Somehow, he would win her over.

"Thank you! I have an idea," he whispered, and kissed Harper's cheek gratefully, ignoring his brother's growl of protest. Tarin only chuckled and hurried away, eager to put things in play.

Chapter 14

Rachel stepped into the ballroom, thinking back to all of those nights with Tarin in this room. Dancing, laughing, swaying to the music until they couldn't stand it anymore. Then their race to his bed and...oh, my. She wanted that back. She wanted to be with him, and dance with him, and...!

"Honey, why do you insist on wearing those awful floral dresses?" Denise sneered. "They haven't been in style for decades."

Rachel swung around, finding her sister in a glorious evening gown of emerald silk that clung to her figure and made her eyes sparkle even more brightly than normal. Her auburn hair was swept up into a sophisticated twist with small curls dancing daintily around her beautiful features which had been made up with an expert hand. Her makeup wasn't heavy, but it enhanced her features perfectly, making Denise look like a delicate angel in emerald green.

Her mother sidled up to them with two glasses of champagne. She handed one to Denise and pointedly ignored Rachel, gazing out over the crowd as if she owned the place.

"You look beautiful, Mother," Rachel murmured, eyeing her mother's gorgeous dress of champagne silk, decorated with an elaborate beaded design along the bodice, and flaring out in champagne colored chiffon to the floor.

Beside them, Rachel felt...invisible. Before, when she'd first seen the flowing, moss green dress with shimmering flowers that had been mysteriously delivered to her, she'd gasped in delight. She'd dressed here at the palace, because she'd had so many things to check on prior to the event tonight. That meant that she'd only had time to pull her hair up into a simple bun. But she'd still felt pretty in the unexpected dress, especially since it had come with a note from Tarin asking her to wear it tonight.

Now, she felt silly and childish. Silly and unsophisticated and invisible.

"I have some things to check on," she told her family, stepping away.

"Yes, go and finish your work, dear. But when we get back to Atlanta, I'll expect you to be more efficient. Never leave things to the last minute."

Rachel stopped and stared at her mother, shocked all over again. Tarin's words earlier today had been filtering through her mind and one word kept coming back to her. "Toxic," she whispered, her lips barely moving.

Denise's turned sharp eyes towards her. "What was that?" she asked, not bothering to hide her sneer. "You really need to speak up, Rachel. Enunciate. No one likes someone who mutters."

Rachel tilted her head, hearing the words, but...she didn't feel her armor crack. She glanced back as she walked away, seeing her mother and her sister bend their heads together as if conspiring, dividing up the room into quadrants, forming a battle plan.

And Rachel didn't doubt that was exactly what they were doing. Watching, she felt another dent in her armor pop back into place. But... it wasn't armor exactly. Was it her confidence?

Turning, she left the ballroom, her family oblivious to her departure. Hell, they were oblivious to her!

Or were they?

The question stopped her in her tracks. She paused, one hand reaching for the wall and she shook her head, trying to bring the thought together. Bullies were insecure people. Her mother and sister were bullies! They were mean and demoralizing and patronizing and...terrible people! She'd known this all her life, but...why would they focus their horrible comments on her? Surely they weren't jealous of her... were they?

The thought was so astounding that she forgot to breathe as she considered the possibility.

"Rachel!" someone called her. It took her a moment to turn and face the person racing towards her. But as she lifted her eyes, her shoulders pulled back, and her lips curled into a smile. Confidence was...heady and powerful! "Yes?" she replied, smiling even more brightly.

The man asked his question and she gave him directions. He moved off, but another person approached. For the next hour, she wandered through the ballroom, the kitchen, and the security office answering questions and ensuring that the gala went off without a hitch.

And the whole time, she thought frantically, trying to figure out what was going on inside her head. And her heart!

One thing she was absolutely certain about...she loved Tarin. And without the haze of humiliation clouding her vision, she suspected that Tarin loved her. Was it possible?

Stepping into the ballroom, her gaze zeroed in on his tall form. Leaning against the doorjamb, she watched, thinking about how he touched her when they were alone, or the way he'd look at her when they were with others. Could that be love?

In that moment, he turned, his eyes searching the crowd. For her? Could he feel her gaze?

Sure enough, he caught her looking at him and she smiled. His eyes warmed and she could see his intent even from this distance.

Everyone was dancing and having a good time, the champagne flowing, tables filled with food and waiters moved among the guests, offering appetizers to those who weren't ready for dinner yet. It was a magical evening and she'd done this, Rachel thought with pride. She'd coordinated this event where everyone was enjoying themselves! It had been her, along with an army of staff, but her ideas and her efforts!

Tarin paused, drinking in her figure in the moss green chiffon dress with the shimmering flowers. She knew that he didn't think her dress was wrong. He'd chosen it and she felt...beautiful.

"Stop it!" her mother hissed, moving to stand beside her. "You're making a fool of yourself!"

Rachel turned slowly to look at her mother, surprised by the acid in her tone.

"Don't worry, Mother," Denise whispered. "I'll stand on her other side. Everyone will assume that he's staring at me. It will be okay."

"I can't believe we still have to protect you like this," her mother grumbled, pasting on a fake smile as she sipped her champagne.

Rachel eyed her sister, watched her preen and pretend to laugh. Why was she laughing? For a moment, Rachel wondered if the rest of the room thought she looked silly too. Or was it just Rachel, seeing her family with new eyes?

"I don't look silly, and I'm not making a fool of myself," she said flatly.

"Don't be ridiculous," her mother snapped.

"He's coming towards us!" Denise hissed. "Shut up and let *me* do the talking."

Rachel didn't even bother to look at her sister. Instead, she focused on Tarin as he came towards her and she shivered at the intent in his eyes. Un-blinded, she saw it. She actually saw the love he felt for her glowing in his eyes!

"Good evening ladies," he said and Rachel dipped into a perfect curtsy.

She felt her mother and sister stare at her, then both of them reacted. Just as Rachel rose from her deep, elegant curtsy, her mother and sister started theirs, fumbling a bit. A curtsy looked easy because the people who knew they'd need to curtsy practiced the movement until it was perfect. But Pamela and Denise were too arrogant and unschooled in palace protocols, so they hadn't bothered to ask what the appropriate greeting was for a member of the royal family.

Rachel watched with silent amusement as her mother and sister tried valiantly to perform an elegant curtsy – and failed! As they rose, she focused her attention on Tarin. "You look very dashing tonight, Your Highness," and her eyes twinkled as she used his title. Rachel even giggled when she heard his growling response.

"And you look exceptionally beautiful, Ms. Morris," he replied in return, just as teasingly formal.

Rachel beamed and started to step closer, intending to whisper in his ear. But Denise elbowed her way between them, forcing Rachel to reel backwards, startled. Rachel heard several gasps from the guests closest who had witnessed the horrible faux pas, but she didn't look around, preferring to rise above and pretend as if her sister hadn't just done something horribly rude.

Tarin, on the other hand, wasn't about to ignore it! "Excuse me, Miss Morris," he said to Denise with an icy frown, "But you just interrupted Rachel. Please step back." His last three words were clipped and succinct.

Denise pulled out her best smile, tilted her head in a coquettish manner, and moved closer. "Look, I know that Rachel is your secretary and you're trying to be nice and all, but she won't mind if we dance. I know she'll understand."

"First of all, Rachel is my project manager, and the best I've ever worked with. She is exceptionally talented and incredibly valuable." He paused, letting his words sink in. "Secondly, don't ever interrupt me or step in front of me." Tarin sighed, obviously striving for patience. "Now, I'd like to speak with Rachel. Step back."

Denise seemed oblivious to his set down and waved a hand dismissively at Rachel. "Oh, just...let her be. She'll shrink away and go find a wall to lean on. Why don't we...?"

"I'm going to dance with Rachel, Miss Morris. If you don't...!"

Denise snickered and looked behind her. "Rachel doesn't dance! She's tried so many times before." Denise turned and looped her arm through Tarin's, rubbing her breast against his arm. "You should have seen her when she tried ballet lessons! She stumbled all over the floor, falling on her face several times. She'd come home covered with bruises and sobbing her heart out! It would have been funny if it wasn't so embarrassing."

"That's a lie," Rachel declared, not angrily, but calmly. With her newfound understanding of Denise, Rachel felt stronger, like she see could see through their subtle as well as not-so-subtle abuse.

Pamela stepped forward, nudging Rachel out of the way. "Of course it's the truth, dear. If you don't remember it that way, then that's your problem." She simpered up at Tarin. "The girl was completely useless on the dance floor, Your Highness. It was amusing, but of course a mother doesn't like to see her daughter in pain, so I stopped her from attending those classes."

"She's actually a beautiful dancer," he announced, extricating his arm from Denise's hold – and not even bothering to be subtle about it.

Denise and Pamela looked stunned, but recovered quickly. "Oh, don't tease. You'll only encourage her."

Tarin moved pointedly away from Denise and reached for Rachel's hand. "Come 'Duteille', we need to talk."

Rachel hesitated, the name "Duteille" sparking memories from that afternoon in Paris. The man...the man trapped in a stone wall, cursed to watch the world pass him by!

"I'm not...." she stopped, then looked at her mother and sister. That's when she laughed. Her mother and sister were literally standing between her and Tarin. They were forming a wall!

"Who is Duteille?" Denise asked. "Is that a nickname you gave to Rachel?" She leaned forward slightly, as if she was about to say something intimate. "She's such a silly girl, isn't she?" She preened for a moment. "If you'd care to dance, Your Highness, *I* would thoroughly enjoy being in your arms."

At that particular moment, the music swelled and the familiar strains hit her. Rachel recognized the music, her eyes widening with surprise and...horror? Yes, a bit of horror, but also a rush of laughter. "No!" she gasped, her eyes widening and she slapped a hand over her mouth, an old habit that she'd thought she'd banished.

"Yes!" Tarin replied with a wicked smile filled with promise, stepping around Denise and taking Rachel's hand. Rachel returned his smile, unaware of the hatred in Denise's gaze or the malevolent look her mother shot at her. Rachel only had eyes for Tarin.

"I'm not good enough yet," she whispered, hesitating as he led her on to the dance floor.

"You're a natural," he countered, and guided her into the crowd of dancers.

At that moment, the music swelled again and Rachel automatically put her hand on his shoulder, sliding her fingers into his. The opening sounds of the Tango surprised everyone and, because it was such a complicated dance, most of the crowd migrated off the dance floor.

Tarin moved forward and she stepped up, staring into his eyes, all the love she felt for him revealed to the occupants of the room. The smile that formed on her face was slow, but unconsciously sexy as she countered and pushed him backwards. Shifting right and left, forward and backwards, to the right, then to the left, spinning and charging, countering...reveling the way the chiffon of her dress floated around her legs. The music and the feel of his hands, the look in his eyes pushed away everything else. In Rachel's mind, there was no audience, no bright lights overhead. In her mind, it was just the two of them and they were naked, in his suite. Every time he pushed, she eased back, but then pushed forward again, defending herself, not allowing him to control her. A moment later, he spun her around and "confusion" reigned, but he caught her in his arms, "confusion" controlled. Again and again, he lunged and she countered, moving to the sound of the music and the feel of his hands. It was just the two of them. Just her, feeling him against her body.

When the dance came to a crescendo, her heart was pounding and she couldn't stop the love from shining in her eyes. Another spin and then...she fell into his arms in a deep dip, his strong body holding her carefully. Safely. He would always catch her, she thought.

The applause was almost deafening as Rachel came back to the present. Tarin pulled her straight, and kept his arm around her waist. The two of them acknowledged the crowd with a nod, and Tarin led her off the dance floor.

Several people stopped them, gushing that Rachel looked amazing out there and asked how she'd learned. "He taught me," she explained to everyone who asked, referring to Tarin as she walked beside him, her hand tucked onto his elbow and his hand over hers, probably to ensure that she stayed there and didn't pull away.

"Goodness, that was amazing!" Harper gushed, hugging Rachel. "I want to learn to dance like that!"

Tarin grinned. "Rachel is a gifted dancer. I'd be happy to teach you too since my big brother is completely inept."

Amit glared at him.

But it was Rachel who gasped her outrage. "You will not!" she yelped, and probably revealed too much when she blushed. Tarin, the rogue, knew exactly what she meant and pulled her in for a hug. "I'll only dance with you, my love."

"You'd better," she grumbled, leaning her head against his shoulder.

"You're mine."

He stilled and looked down at her, his eyes unreadable as he said, "Come with me."

Rachel didn't have a chance to protest since he dragged her out of the ballroom. Because there were so many people everywhere, it was difficult to find a private space, but eventually, he found an empty room and pulled her inside, slamming the door behind them. "Am I?" he demanded.

Rachel was completely out of breath, not just from the frantic race out of the ballroom, but also from the heated look in his eyes. "Are you what?" she asked. She reached out, needing the comfort of his touch.

"Am I yours?" he demanded, moving closer, pulling her flush against him.

She held her breath as she stared up at him. "I want you to be mine," she admitted. "I've been such a fool this week, but I don't want to be Duteille any longer. I don't want to be frozen in my life, just watching the world pass me by." She lifted up onto her toes and kissed him gently. "I want to be all the way in," she concluded, and waited for his response.

"It's about time!" he groaned, wrapping his arms around her and spinning her around, kissing her with all of the pent up passion that he'd tried to ignore while she'd been with her family.

When he put her back on the floor, they were both panting. "I don't want you around your family, if you can even call those people that, anymore. You have a new family. Starting now!"

"Okay," she said, beaming up at him.

"That means marriage, Rachel. I want my ring on your finger!" He dug into his pocket and produced a stunning diamond ring. "If you accept this, it means more than just our engagement. It means that you'll be with me forever. And you'll recognize how bad your family is and get rid of them. I'm serious, your mother and sister are evil and your father is weak, allowing them to do whatever to him. You need and deserve so much more than that."

"Okay," she replied, stunning them both.

His eyes widened, then narrowed as he looked down at her. "Okay? Just...okay?"

She laughed. "You're right, Tarin. I've been letting them manipulate me for too long. I can't let it continue. And..." she blushed, but his hands tightened around her waist, giving her courage. "Well, if we have children, I don't want my family to..."

She couldn't finish again because he kissed her. She melted into his kiss and she wanted to laugh and cry and scream with happiness. She felt liberated! For the first time in so long, she was completely and amazingly free! She hadn't realized until this moment how much her family dragged her down. But it was time to break free from that toxicity and find her happiness. They'll just have to survive without her and, whatever happens to their business, would happen because of their ineptitude.

"I love you," he murmured against her lips.

"I love you too," she replied, kissing him with all of the love she felt in her heart.

Epilogue

"I'm going!" she announced in a tone that brooked no argument.

Tarin followed her out of the dressing room, his eyes focused on her back instead of...well, the rest of her because looking at the rest of her just drove him wild with lust. He couldn't think about...*that*...right now.

"You're *not* going!" he countered, his tone absolute.

Rachel slowly turned around, pulling the dress over her eight and a half month pregnant belly and hiding the pretty red bra she'd pulled on moments ago. Her panties didn't match because the panties that matched the bra were now too small for her pregnant body, but Rachel knew that Tarin still desired her. The evidence was pretty clear if she just looked down.

This argument couldn't be resolved with sex though. So she didn't look. She kept her eyes upwards.

"Tarin, this is the opening ceremony for the university center. You've been working on this project for years and I'm proud of you! I'm going! I'm standing by your side and I'm going to be clapping harder than anyone else."

He rubbed a hand over the back of his neck. "But you're pregnant, Rachel!"

Rachel laughed. "Yes. I noticed!" she replied softly. Moving closer, she rested her hands on his chest, tilting her head back to look into his face. "Tarin, we've been married for two years now. And you've been working on this center the whole time. I'm going to this ceremony. I *will* be with you."

"I want you here, resting with your feet up and eating something nutritious," he countered, his hands caressing her belly.

She covered his hands with hers, loving him so much that it overwhelmed her sometimes. "I'll be fine. Besides, if anything happens, the university is only two miles from the hospital. I love you and this is your moment. I *have* to be there."

He moved closer, leaning forward to kiss her. "Fine. But if anything happens, you'll tell me, right?"

She grinned cheekily up at him. "You'll be the first to know," she vowed.

Tarin sighed, closing his eyes as he accepted the inevitability of her attendance. He didn't like it, but one thing he'd come to love about her was her determination. It was sexy as hell and he loved her more with each passing day!

Six hours later, Rachel beamed and clapped so hard that her hands stung as Tarin cut the giant ribbon with a pair of shining scissors. The crowd roared and stood up, but Rachel was in too much pain to stand. Thankfully, no one noticed as they surged forward, eager to offer their congratulations.

Still, Rachel waited for another thirty minutes. The crowd had finally thinned out by then, most people moving over to the food tables and mingling around the atrium of the main building for the new university campus.

Finally, Tarin turned and saw her. She'd stayed in her chair, her hands covering her round tummy. But he didn't notice her beauty. He only saw how pale she was.

"Rachel!" he roared, moving over to her and bending down to peer into her eyes.

"What's wrong, love?" he demanded.

She lifted one finger, silently asking him to hold on a moment. When the contraction eased, she took a deep breath, her shoulders relaxing, and she gave him a genuine smile.

"Oh my, that was a bad one," she admitted. "Would you mind taking me to the hospital now?" she asked, her tone utterly casual.

Tarin was so stunned, he almost fell. Thankfully, he recovered and stood up, calling out to his guards even though they could see what was happening and were already arranging for transport to the hospital. Tarin scooped her up into his arms and carried her out of the building, ignoring the curious crowd.

It would be reported in the news the following day that the hand-some prince groaned quietly as he put his wife into the vehicle. But the greatest news was that the royal family of Raminar had a new baby boy in their happy family. Mother and son were thriving and the royal family was thrilled to add a new member. It was also reported that the Princess Rachel's side of the family was still struggling to recover from their bankruptcy filings and her parents' divorce was final.

Message from Elizabeth:
I sincerely hope that you enjoyed Tarin and Rachel's story! I know
that you have an incredibly busy life, but reviews are hugely important.
Would you take just a few seconds to leave a review? Just a few words are
extremely helpful! Thank you so much!
(If you don't want to leave feedback in a public forum, feel free to e-mail
me directly at elizabeth@elizabethlennox.com. I answer all e-mails per-
sonally, although it sometimes takes me a while. Please don't be offended
if I don't respond immediately. I tend to lose myself in writing stories and
have a hard time pulling my head out of the book.)

Keep scrolling for a titillating excerpt from my next series Forsaken
Sons first book One More Kiss!

Excerpt for One More Kiss
Release date: March 12, 2021

"I need your help."

Kinsley looked up from the receipt she was trying to decipher. For the past week, she'd been squinting at receipts, pulling her hair out in an effort to determine how to associate each cost to the projects.

So when he poked his head into her office, it took Kinsley a long moment to shift gears. "I'm sorry?"

He waved his hand. "Leave all that. I need your help with something."

Kinsley grabbed a pen and notebook, and obediently followed behind Lincoln. "How can I help?" she asked, excited for a distraction after working in her office all week with no interruptions other than phone calls from reporters and investors asking, demanding, threatening, and terrorizing her in their efforts to speak with Lincoln Meyers. One person had literally threatened an FBI investigation on her if she didn't bring the man to the phone immediately. At that time, Lincoln hadn't even been in the building...at least, she hadn't seen him that morning. But...that wasn't out of the ordinary. Some days, she didn't see him at all, although he'd leave instructions on her desk.

He fascinated her and the more she learned about him, the more she... liked. If her boyfriend became angry when she refused to tell him anything about her new, mysterious employer or what she was doing for the famous recluse, it didn't bother Kinsley in the least. She considered guarding his privacy part of her job.

"Kinsley!" he bellowed.

Kinsley glared at his back from her doorway. "I'm not a dog, Mr. Meyers," she snapped. "And I'm right here, waiting for instruction. No need to bellow when a kind word will suffice."

He stopped and looked over his shoulder at her. Did his gaze move over her figure? Kinsley wasn't sure.

"I'm well aware of that fact." He turned and headed out the door, disappearing into one of the rare sunny days in Seattle.

Kinsley followed at a more leisurely pace. She wasn't racing after a man who hollered at her. No way!

When she stepped outside, he was already sitting on his motorcycle, strapping his helmet on. "Here," he handed a helmet to her. "Put this on and climb on."

Kinsley blinked at the helmet in her hands, not sure what he meant. "Why would I put this on?"

"Because I need your help. Come on."

She eyed the bike, then at his massive back that was literally rippling with muscles underneath a white tee shirt. Swallowing, she shook her head, stepping back from the bike. "Nope. I don't ride motorcycles. Do you know what the death rate on motorcycles is these days?"

He chuckled. "I'm very well aware of the death rate. Which is why I need your help."

Again, she shook her head, tucking the helmet underneath her arm. "Nope. No way!"

He chuckled. "Fine. Drive your little Prius over to the track." A moment later, he was off, zipping down the driveway towards the mysterious area she'd wondered about.

For a long moment, Kinsley stared after him, not sure if she should follow him down that mysterious road, or head back into her office to figure out the zillions of seemingly random receipts. Eventually, curiosity got the better of her. She was eager to spend a little time outside of those four, harshly white walls. Hurrying back around the building, she grabbed her keys and drove around the building in the direction Lincoln had gone.

Sure enough, he'd parked the motorcycle next to what looked like a huge racetrack. It even banked at the ends, presumably for safety when a vehicle rounded those corners. Huh! The guy owned a racetrack! That was new. She'd heard of home theaters or basketball courts, private exercise rooms, even a special studio in one's house for yoga. The rich and famous tended to be an odd breed. But none of the articles she'd read included a racetrack on a wealthy person's estate.

"Okay, I'm here. How can I help?"

He was attaching something to the motorcycle, using a wrench and a few other tools that Kinsley didn't recognize. "Grab a pair of headphones from that box over there and put them on. I'll be talking to you through the speaker connected to my helmet. You'll need to time and log the various intervals I'll give you." He stood up and Kinsley's eyes moved down over his long, muscular legs, her mouth going a bit dry.

Stop staring at his legs, she scolded herself. But her eyes drifted upward, taking in his thigh muscles. And his arms. The tee shirt had short sleeves, so she could see the bulging muscles in his arms. The triceps twitched every time he turned the wrench, mesmerizing her.

Blinking hard, she forced her gaze away and peered in the direction he'd pointed. There was a box filled with headphones and other strange equipment, a tangled mess of speakers and wires and odd things poking out of the box that didn't seem to have anything to do with headphones.

She walked over and pulled at something that looked like a single headphone set, unraveling the wires to release the headset. "What am I timing?"

"Me," he said as he swung his leg over the motorcycle, kicked the stand out of the way and revved the engine. Sliding the helmet back over his head, he glanced over at her, nodding towards the headsets again.

Quickly, Kinsley put the headphones on, then stepped closer when he motioned for her forward.

He reached out to adjust the microphone, his touch making her skin tingle, then flipped a switch under her right ear. She shivered, and tried to pretend she hadn't.

"Can you hear me now?"

His deep, sexy voice came right through to her ear. She nodded, feeling that tingling sensation envelop her.

"Say something so that I can test your microphone, to make sure that you're connected to me as well."

Despite the rumbling of his motorcycle engine, Kinsley could hear him clearly through the head set. "Is this okay?"

He grinned and winked at her. "Perfect."

Kinsley managed not to shiver again, but it was more of a struggle than she'd care to admit.

When he finally turned away, Kinsley breathed a sigh of relief.

Her relief was short-lived as she watched Lincoln speed off down the track. "Time the laps, Kinsley," she heard through her head set. "Make sure that you capture the time as I go over the yellow line on the track."

Kinsley looked in the box and found a stopwatch, carefully untangling the cord. "Okay, ready. Tell me when to start."

A chuckle echoed through the connection. "How about when I rounded that last corner."

"Too late," she shot back, grinning at his playful tone.

"That's not very efficient, Kinsley."

She shook her head, smiling even though he couldn't see her. "Listen, buddy, I've been threatened by about ten different people this week because I wouldn't let them talk to you. So don't even try to intimidate me now."

"Who threatened you?" he asked.

The question sounded conversational, but Kinsley heard a note of anger as well. "Don't worry about it," she replied, glancing up at the man speeding across the racetrack, then back down at the stopwatch. "I handled it."

"Give me a name, Kinsley," he growled.

"What are you going to do? And would you *please* slow down? You're heading into that corner too fast!"

He laughed again, and sped up. In fact, he took the corner so fast, and angled the motorcycle so low as he leaned into the turn, that she held her breath in alarm.

"I'm fine," she heard him say when he came out of the turn. "Give me a name."

"Concentrate on what you're doing. I'm timing your laps."

He laughed again, and stopped interrogating her. Hopefully, he was concentrating on what he was doing. Unfortunately, so was Kinsley and every time he came up to the U of the race track, he seemed to be going faster, taking the corner at a slightly deeper angle. It terrified her every time, but she forced herself to capture the lap times.

After about forty-five minutes, he drove up to where she was standing, and trembling, and took off his helmet. "What do you think?"

She glared at him. "What do *I* think?! I think you're insane! I think you need to slow down! I think you almost –"

He chuckled. "I'm fine, Kinsley," he assured her. He bent over the motorcycle and the sight of those strong muscles flexing under his jeans made her mind sputter to a stop. He straightened up, something in his hands, and looked back at her. "You don't know this yet, but I'm *very* careful."

He walked over to the box and put something else in while Kinsley sputtered her surprise. "*Careful?*" She moved closer, tugging the headset off. "How in the world were you careful? You were speeding around that track at...like...*fast!*"

He laughed. "Were you worried about me?"

"Yes!" she yelled, throwing her hands in the air.

"Would you have been upset if I'd crashed?" He asked teasingly.

The blush that stole over her cheeks was enchanting. "Yes!" she replied, but not as vehemently. In fact, it was barely a whisper.